"Ace, I was sur̶ ̶ ̶ ̶ ̶ ̶ ̶ ̶ ̶ ̶ ̶ ̶ ̶ ̶ ̶ ̶ ̶ ̶ ̶e confided in Gram a̶ Her dark eyes met h̶ ̶ ̶ ̶ ̶ ̶ ̶ ̶ ̶ ̶ ̶ ̶ ̶ ̶ ̶ ̶ ̶ ̶ hard at the concern in them.

He sighed deeply. Would they ever get past this Aunt Millie thing? "Nicole, it really doesn't matter. I accepted the whole business a long time ago. I've learned to live with it. Fact is, I never think about it unless someone brings it up."

Her eyes flickered. Or perhaps only the light through the west window caught in them. "I think it matters."

"How so?"

"I think it's made you afraid of getting close to people."

"Who says I'm afraid?" He closed the distance between them. If she wanted proof to the contrary, he could provide it here and now. He brushed the back of his fingers along her cheek.

He shouldn't have done it.

The jolt that burned down his arm went straight to his heart, threatening locks on doors he didn't intend to open. The look in her eyes—intense, uncertain—twisted like a suddenly discovered key.

Forget the locks.

Forget the promises he'd made and kept these past dozen or more years.

Only one thing mattered: He wanted her in his arms.

He reached for her, but she stepped away, suddenly very interested in the framed sampler he'd leaned against the wall.

LINDA FORD and her husband raised a family of fourteen children, ten adopted, providing her plenty of opportunity to experience God's love and faithfulness. One of her goals in writing is to reveal a little of God's wondrous love through the lives of the people in her stories. She lives in Alberta, Canada, on a ranch she shares with her husband, a paraplegic client, boomerang children, and adorable visiting grandchildren.

Books by Linda Ford

Don't miss out on any of our super romances. Write to us at the following address for information on our newest releases and club information.

Heartsong Presents Readers' Service
PO Box 721
Uhrichsville, OH 44683

Or visit www.heartsongpresents.com

Cry
of My Heart

Linda Ford

Heartsong Presents

Dedicated to the Canadian Peacekeepers who risk their lives around the world, and to their families who stay at home and wait for their return. My prayers for your safety and peace of mind.

A note from the Author:
I love to hear from my readers! You may correspond with me by writing:

Linda Ford
Author Relations
PO Box 721
Uhrichsville, OH 44683

ISBN 1-59789-059-6

CRY OF MY HEART

one

She knew it was an answer to prayer—just not the one she'd expected. She hadn't seen Andrew Conners since she was ten and he twelve, and she had no desire to see him now. Not after the way he'd treated his aunt. Only God seemed to have sent this opportunity her way, so she marched down the alley and through the gate into the yard next door.

Standing on the step, facing the door, she smoothed her hands over the hips of her pink cotton pants and tugged at the hem of her matching floral blouse. Maybe she just thought it seemed like an answer to prayer because it fit her needs so perfectly.

God, if I'm mistaken, have him not be here.

She hadn't even said amen, hadn't even knocked, when the door jerked open, and she stared at a pair of arms clutching a large box. The box-carrying figure halted, turned, and regarded her with wide, startled hazel eyes. Slowly he lowered the box to the floor, and they stared at each other.

Her mouth fell open. She knew he wouldn't be the kid he'd been eighteen years ago, but somehow she hadn't thought he'd be so. . .so big. He had to be over six feet tall. Power and authority practically oozed from him. His blue jeans were faded, his black T-shirt smudged with patches of dust. His skin glowed golden; his brown hair shone with streaks.

She swallowed, her throat strangely stiff. This was Andrew? She remembered a scrawny, sometimes sad, sometimes angry boy. The only thing reminiscent of that person was his eyes. A smile flashed across his face, making those hazel eyes suddenly warm.

"Nicole Costello. I'd have known you anywhere."

Nicole tried to ignore the way her heart tripped over itself several times in her assessment of this man, leaving her as scatterbrained as her younger sister, Carrie, without the excuse of being seventeen years old.

"Hi, Andrew."

He quirked one eyebrow. "Make it Ace. I haven't gone by Andrew since—" He shrugged. "In a very long time."

"And it's Nicole Thomas now."

"You're married then?"

"No. My mom remarried Paul Thomas."

He snapped his fingers. "I remember. They got engaged that Christmas I was here, didn't they?"

She nodded, surprised he remembered. Surprised he even remembered how to get to small-town Reliance, Montana.

"So you've decided to come back?" She heard the way her voice grated with disapproval and hoped he wouldn't notice.

"You sound. . ." He paused before he said, "Surprised."

"It's too late, Andrew. Years and years too late." A tremor skated across her shoulders at the way his expression hardened. "You didn't even come for the funeral."

His eyes lost their warmth, and she knew if she'd hoped for an explanation she was going to be disappointed. But it was so sad. Aunt Millie wasn't even a relative of hers, only Gram's best friend for decades. She and Carrie and Gram were the closest thing to family Aunt Millie had in her declining years.

He fixed her with an assessing stare. "I remember you as a kid who said what she thought. I see you haven't changed."

She would like to tell him what she really thought, but it might not be conducive to the business she hoped to conduct. "I understand you're interested in selling the contents of the house." She handed him her business card. "I'd like to buy some things."

Not even glancing at it, he dropped the card in his breast pocket before he stepped aside and waved her in. "I'm anxious to be done and out of here. Anything in particular you're interested in?"

"Some of the antiques, if you're selling them."

"I'm getting rid of everything."

She wanted to protest the way he talked—like it was nothing more than stuff—instead of the remnants of his aunt's life. As she stepped inside the house a pang of emptiness touched her heart. She stood in the wide kitchen where she'd many times visited Aunt Millie.

Open-flapped boxes teetered along one wall. A cupboard over the sink stood ajar as if Andrew had been cleaning it out. The whole place smelled old and closed in.

She touched the chipped brown teapot on the table. "This was Aunt Millie's favorite."

"It's seen better days," he muttered.

"She said it made the best tea."

Andrew grunted impatiently. "It would make good landfill."

Nicole stopped smiling. It seemed every mention of Aunt Millie caused him to become increasingly defensive.

"And how are your parents?" he asked, as if hoping to divert her from the protest on her lips.

Nicole froze inside. It still hit her like a jolt. She stared at the label on a box. "They were killed in a car accident seven years ago. Carrie, Gram—Grandmother—and I are all that's left." If only they hadn't gone on that holiday. One minute they were full of excitement and joy. The next, gone, their lives destroyed by a swerving vehicle on a steep mountain grade. And in that moment, life for Nicole had taken a sharp turn. In her third year at university she'd quit to come home and help Gram raise Carrie. Only her faith in God sustained her.

"I'm sorry," he said. "Tough break."

Nicole relaxed, letting a gentle smile curve her lips. "It hasn't been too bad. I still have Gram and my sister, Carrie." Taking a deep breath, she faced him squarely. "What about you? I remember you and your mom were going to move in with Aunt Millie. You had such dreams. You were going to follow God and be a Christian soldier. I remember we talked about it for hours. And then nothing. As if you disappeared off the face of the earth."

His smile receded, but the quick masking of the expression in his eyes riveted her attention on his face. "Sometimes life interferes with our plans."

"For sure." What details had shaped his life since she'd last seen him? Not that anything could excuse his neglect of Aunt Millie. "Andrew, I—"

"Ace. Andrew's someone from my past." His hard tone made it clear he would tolerate no argument.

"All right. Ace then. Have you had a chance to go through the house?"

"Five bedrooms, a dining room, living room, pantry, and store room." He ticked off his fingers as he spoke. "Not to mention a basement I haven't dared venture into. All crammed with stuff."

She hoped she didn't look too pleased at his distress. "You've forgotten the garage and the attic."

"An attic?" He rolled his eyes and moaned.

She nodded. Maybe by the time he got through it all he'd have an inkling of what he'd missed in ignoring his aunt.

He lifted his arms in defeat. "Good thing I don't have anything urgent on my calendar." He sighed. "You're welcome to go through and pick out whatever you want."

"Oh, but not until you've had a chance to decide what you want to keep."

He shrugged. "I can't think I'd want anything. I'm not much for sentimentality."

"But Aunt Millie thought so much of you. Surely you want something to remember her by." Again that hard, closed look came to his eyes.

"Take whatever you want."

She curled her fingers. How could he be so unfeeling? As if nothing about Aunt Millie mattered?

"About the attic—I don't recall seeing an entrance."

Nicole nodded. "I'd better show you." She led the way through the living room, up the stairs to the back bedroom crowded with boxes, a huge wardrobe, an old-fashioned sewing machine, and other pieces of furniture. "You really do have your job cut out for you." For the first time she felt a touch of sympathy. "It can't be easy disposing of your aunt's things."

Again that sudden flash in his eyes. "It's only a job."

Her rush of sympathy flared into anger. "I heard your mother had died. I'm sorry. That left Aunt Millie as your last living relative. I'd think she deserved a little more regret or sorrow on your part."

"She was old and crippled even when I saw her last. I'm sure she'd suffered enough."

Against her will, Nicole was forced to agree. "I suppose I

meant sorrow for what you've lost. Your family. That has to mean something."

The corners of his mouth drew down. "Family! What's that? Only people related by accident of birth."

She faced him squarely. "Family is a whole lot more than that." She realized her fists were planted on her hips and dropped her arms to her sides. " 'Course you only get out of family what you put into it." He'd put nothing into his. He'd get nothing back.

His scowl deepened. "Meaning?"

She slowed her breathing. "Some people don't value what they have." She felt the heat from his eyes as he stared at her without answering. She turned away. "Let me show you the attic."

❧

Ace watched Nicole yank open the double closet doors and flip a latch in the ceiling. He remembered her as an intense, skinny kid with a mane of long black hair. Her hair was no longer waist length, but she didn't seem to have lost any of her intensity. Her emotions vibrated from her. Sharp disapproval. Directed at him. Condemning him for what she saw as his failure to live up to her expectations. Huh! Fat lot she knew about it.

He shrugged. He'd learned to ignore all sorts of prejudice. He leaned against the wall where he could study her as she fiddled with a curl of rope.

An attractive bit of humanity. Small boned. Tiny stature. Ace let his gaze linger on her short, pixie-cut dark hair. He liked the way it emphasized her delicate features. Her olive skin, inherited from her Italian father, glowed with health.

No doubt she'd told him what happened to her father. But

it was so long ago he couldn't remember. A freak accident or something. Then she'd lost both her mother and stepfather. Tough break for someone who valued family so much.

She tugged on the rope she'd managed to untangle. A patch of ceiling rolled back, and a set of stairs unfolded at her feet. She coughed at the cloud of dust sifting over her, brushed herself off, and faced him. "Ta-da." She grinned and swept her arm up the steps. "The attic."

Ace's gaze lingered on her wide smile before he turned to stare into the dim overhead room. Why did he get the feeling she enjoyed his annoyance over the task ahead of him? She probably figured it served him right for not keeping in touch with Aunt Millie.

"Go ahead," she urged. "It's full of treasures."

"I'll bet." If the rest of the house were any indication, the attic would be crowded to the rafters.

She waited for him to lead the way and pointed to a pull chain for the light as he stepped to the board floor.

It was even worse than he'd imagined. Rows of old coats hung from wires. Boxes crowded under the eaves. Trunks, bookcases loaded with junk, and more boxes everywhere he looked.

"Great," he muttered. "A veritable gold mine."

Nicole stepped around him. "Before I grew up and left home, I used to come up here every year to help Aunt Millie get her Christmas decorations."

"Grew up? I don't think so." He held his hand out a little above waist height to indicate her short stature.

She sniffed and tilted her chin. "Gram says good things come in small packages."

"So does nitro."

Her chuckle rolled across his mind. "Let's hope the comparison doesn't mean anything." She turned to glance around the room. "There're the Christmas decorations. Right where she always had me put them." She picked her way around several boxes, an old leather trunk, and a crooked footstool with stuffing bulging out of ripped seams, to a stack of boxes marked *C'mas decorations*. Kneeling, she pushed aside the boxes. "Look—here are the outdoor ones." She held up a wire frame shaped like an angel then turned to stare at a wooden crèche scene. "She loved decorating for the season."

Most Christmases passed without Ace even noticing, but watching the play of emotions on Nicole's face he could understand why it had been important, and probably enjoyable, for Aunt Millie. Seeing Nicole's pleasure, he could almost imagine himself liking the idea of stringing lights and decorating a tree. Then he jerked his thoughts into submission. He didn't need Christmas or lights or even neighbors like Nicole and her sister and grandmother. He was happy with things the way they were.

Nicole shoved aside the wise men and pulled out a life-size plastic reindeer. "I'd forgotten about this." Turning to face Ace, she sat back on her heels. "Do you remember it?"

For one unguarded moment Ace recalled the excitement, the promise, the hope he'd felt when Aunt Millie bought that decoration, and then he snapped the gate shut on his memories. There would be no more wishing and wondering. No more false hopes. "Vaguely," he answered.

Nicole's expression sobered, and she studied him as if expecting more response. "Aunt Millie would never let me bring it down. She said it was yours and she was saving it for you. She told me when you came back you could put it up yourself." She tipped her head. "Ace, what happened to you? Why didn't you come back?"

Ace wished he'd never allowed her to show him the attic. "It's ancient history." But her pixie face screwed up, and he knew she wasn't going to accept his answer even before she shook her head and spoke.

"Not that ancient. Besides, I guess I want to"—she shook her head again as if troubled by her thoughts—"I want to understand what happened." She pushed the reindeer toward him.

He touched the red nose of the ornament and remembered how it had blinked off and on when the electric cord hanging from its neck was plugged in. He shoved the silly plastic animal aside and straightened until his head almost touched the low ceiling.

He'd succeeded in leaving behind that part of his life. He didn't need little Miss Nicole bringing it up. Crossing his arms over his chest, he said, "I doubt I could add anything to what Aunt Millie said."

"That's the strange thing. After you left, all she could talk about was you and your mother coming to stay. And then" —an enigmatic lift of one shoulder—"she just clammed up. Whenever I asked her what happened, she would get a real sad look on her face. Sometimes I caught a glimpse of tears in her eyes. I know she prayed for you, and I expect part of her prayers was for you to come back."

Ace stared past her. He focused on a broken coat tree, leaning drunkenly to the left. He had no intention whatsoever of delving into his past, revealing secrets, unveiling his heart. "I'll need to get a truck in here to haul this stuff away."

She shifted as she looked across the room. "I wondered if

maybe your mother found a new boyfriend, and that's why. . ." Her voice trailed off as if she expected him to supply the answer.

He heard the invitation in her voice, and his chest tightened. *I'm not spilling my guts.*

"But you never came. I waited for you. I thought you'd come."

Her voice said it all. Her disappointment with him. Her opinion that he'd failed. She looked so concerned. He remembered this uncanny thing about her. How, even at ten, her frank, wide-eyed, caring look made him tell her things he'd thought were locked securely inside his heart. But now, older and wiser, he knew how to keep his secrets behind barred doors where they couldn't hurt him. He'd tell her only enough to relieve her misconceptions.

"No new boyfriend. My mother died that same year." She'd hit the bottle again and was ashamed to let Aunt Millie know. "When I was thirteen." What would she say if he told her how his mother had died? Downing one mickey after another until she passed out. Not an unusual occurrence by any means. But this time the blood alcohol was too much for her body to take.

"I heard she died. How awful. But then why didn't you come live with Aunt Millie? It would seem the natural thing to do."

"You'd think." He made no attempt to hide his sarcasm.

After the doctor's blunt announcement that his mother had drunk herself to death, Ace sat across a big mahogany desk and watched the doctor punch in the phone number that brought a social worker to the room.

For weeks, while he was shifted from the emergency shelter to a group home and then to the first of a series of foster homes, Ace clung to the hope that Aunt Millie would come for him. She'd promised they would live with her.

But she never came.

"I guess a teenage boy without his mother was more than she cared to deal with."

Nicole pinched her lips together briefly before she spoke. "No way. Aunt Millie wouldn't turn away anyone."

Except me. He pushed the pain back, behind a lifetime of walls.

"Why didn't you call her? Seems you could have at least let her know you were okay."

Her suggestion that he'd turned his back on Aunt Millie stung. "What makes you think I didn't? Fact is, I sent her a half dozen letters. I even managed to sneak in a few phone calls, but all she said was she'd get back to me." He shrugged, proving to himself it no longer mattered. "She never called, and she never came. And I quit bugging her." He'd shut Aunt Millie out of his life after that. Permanently.

Nicole rocked her head back and forth. "I just know there's more to it." Her eyes narrowed and darkened with intensity as she brought her gaze back to him.

He remained perfectly still, meeting her look steadily, knowing the least shifting of his eyes or even a fiddling of his fingers would provide clues to his emotional state he didn't wish her to see. Didn't even want to own.

She edged over to perch on an old trunk and, leaning her elbows on her knees, nodded. "Okay, tell me everything from when I last saw you."

"What?"

"Yup. Where you lived. How you felt. What was going through your mind? What you do now. How your relationship with God has grown—"

At her probing questions, tension grabbed the back of his head, making his scalp too tight. But he would not let her interest dent the protective shell he'd built around his emotions. He uncurled his fingers, rolled his head back and forth, then held up one hand. "Enough. You haven't changed a bit, have you?"

"Maybe. Maybe not. I guess I'm still curious."

"You think?" But even at ten it hadn't been idle curiosity. Even then she'd managed to get him to tell her his hope for a permanent home, his dreams for the future. Maybe her intense way of listening made him open up. Maybe her attitude said it mattered. Whatever. It held the same power today to unlock his thoughts. But today was different. He was different. He'd learned to guard his feelings. But knowing she wouldn't let him get away with saying nothing, he told her briefly of living in a steady stream of foster homes.

"I know I wasn't an easy kid."

"Umm. I can imagine your tough-guy act."

"How would you know?"

"You had a good start on it even back then."

"You saw that?"

She smiled. "Not really. But I remember my mom saying you thought you could protect yourself with what she called 'attitude.'"

"Yeah, well, my attitude was well honed by the time I was eighteen and out of the system."

"And then what?"

"I qualified for a scholarship, went to university, and took my degree in petroleum engineering. Worked on offshore drilling rigs for several years."

"And now?"

"Still in the petroleum industry. Only now I say when and where."

"And that's important, isn't it?"

"Saying when and where? You bet it is."

"Still. It's too bad."

"Too bad I'm more or less my own boss?"

"Not that. That's great if it's what you want. But you and Aunt Millie—the last of your family. Such a waste."

"I guess you don't miss what you never had."

She looked thoughtful. Was she as unconvinced as he? When her mouth made a little round shape and her eyes widened, he wondered what new idea darted across her mind.

"Here I am talking as if Aunt Millie was your only family. How stupid of me. You probably have a wife and kids by now."

"Not me. I've been far too busy."

She considered him unblinkingly for several seconds as if trying to discover what hidden message might lie behind his words. "And God?"

"You might say He's on the back burner." Way back. So far back he never thought of Him anymore. God, Aunt Millie, and hopes—all part of a childhood dream lasting one short Christmas season.

❧

Shock waves washed through Nicole's thoughts. How could he shove God away? Especially when he had no family. No one to love. As unthinkable as being at sea without a boat. She thanked God daily for His love and her family. "I can't imagine. To me, God and family are the most important things in the world."

"So I gathered." He pushed to his feet making it clear he didn't want to continue this discussion. "Come on. Let's get out of here."

She took a long, lingering look around the low room. She could almost see Aunt Millie bent over a box poking through the contents, her grumbling voice worrying over some item she couldn't locate. Nicole took a deep breath. Past the odor of mothballs and dust she caught a whiff of the rosewater and glycerin soap Aunt Millie used. Her throat tightened as she turned to follow Ace down the steep steps.

They came to a halt in the kitchen.

He took her business card from his breast pocket. "Grandpa's Attic. Nice name."

"It was my grandfather's store. Gram let me take it over and restore it."

He continued reading. " 'An eclectic art gallery. Something for everyone.' Sounds interesting. And you'd like to add antiques to your collection?"

She nodded. "I look for unusual and quality items. Aunt Millie had some wonderful things."

"Take whatever you can use," Ace said.

She licked at one corner of her mouth and tasted the dust from the attic. This was where things got difficult. What she wanted and what she could afford were two different things. She'd like to pack it all over to her storeroom. Every last dish, knickknack, and picture. Everything except what he should keep. But she'd spent the last of her savings on renovating the store and then on a buying trip to Great Falls.

Her business had proved moderately successful. She'd learned a lot. She understood she had three distinct demographics of buyers. The tourists who wanted something they could carry away in their purses or have shipped. Something reminiscent of the area. Then there were the decorators looking for signature feature pieces. For them the price was secondary to original, interesting, eye-catching appeal. The last group was the serious collectors who were willing to pay significant amounts for quality work. She knew the sort of thing that appealed to each group. If she could offer more stock—some truly unique and wonderful things—she could raise her profits significantly.

Right now she managed to pay the bills but with nothing left over. She couldn't continue at that level of income. There were always emergencies to plan for, like car repairs and family needs. And then Carrie would be graduating in a year. Their parents' life insurance had been meant for university, but with rising costs Carrie would require a whole lot more than the life insurance proceeds. First on her list of needs, though, was Gram's cataract surgery. The doctor had warned it would soon be necessary, and Nicole wanted the operation done at the best clinic available. She had to earn the funds.

If she could get some of Aunt Millie's things cleaned and on display, she would be able to take advantage of the busy tourist season.

"What's the matter? Have you changed your mind?"

"No. But there is a problem. I can't afford to pay what they're worth."

"So don't tell me what they're worth, and I won't know."

"That's just plain dumb." She glared at him. "I'll pay a reasonable price for whatever I take."

"Okay. What are you suggesting?"

"I'm hoping you'll agree to let me have them on consignment." She rushed ahead before he could refuse. "I'll give you a modest down payment. We'll make a thorough list of all the items I take and set a price for them. Then when I sell them I pay you. Okay?"

He shrugged. "Not a problem. I just want to get rid of it. I'm not worried about the money."

He said it like a man who didn't need to worry about where the next dollar came from. Of course he had no responsibilities. No family who depended on him.

She had Gram and Carrie.

"I *am* concerned about money," she said. Unlike him she couldn't afford to make decisions without considering the consequences.

"Suit yourself. I'm glad to let you have whatever you want. This stuff probably means something to you." He gave an encompassing wave around the room. "It means nothing to me except how to move it."

She stared at him with disbelief. "Some of Aunt Millie's stuff is priceless. You should at least make sure you get a fair deal."

He grinned. "You mean to say you antique dealers aren't above taking advantage of a person's ignorance?"

"I can't speak for anyone else, but I'd offer what I considered fair." Why did it all come down to money? So much more was at stake here. Family. Memories. Tradition. Aunt Millie had told her about things that had been in the family for generations. They should be kept there. "You need to go through and pick out what you'll want to keep. Like the collection of brass elephants that came from India with some ancestor of yours. Aunt Millie's great-uncle, I believe it was. And the cut-glass dishes, a wedding present to your great-great-grandparents. Aunt Millie said those dishes were the only thing to survive a tornado."

His expression had grown distant. "I'm sure some of the stuff has a fascinating history. And no doubt telling your customers will up your chances of a sale."

"But some are family heirlooms. You should keep the things that meant so much to Aunt Millie."

Again that hard, closed look to his eyes. "Don't you think we're a little past that?"

"But she was—"

"Family. I know. You've already mentioned it several times. But, honestly, don't you think family means more to you than it did to her?"

"How can you say that? As if Aunt Millie didn't care?" She shook her head.

"Come on, Nicole. If family was so important to her, don't you think she would have done things differently?"

"You mean she would have brought you here to live?"

He gave her a steady look. "What do you think?"

"I don't know what happened, but there has to be an explanation, because Aunt Millie did care about you. I'll prove it somehow. She deserves the truth, and so do you."

"Be careful that the truth isn't more than you want to know."

She returned look for look. No way was she afraid of the truth. "It's not me who's been running for eighteen years."

"Running? Who was running?"

"You, and I think you know it. The question is, what are you running from? Are you afraid of what you might find if you go back to the beginning? To the time before things fell apart for you?"

"Ah, I see you've been studying psychology. Or is that wisdom from a women's magazine?"

She smiled. It didn't take a psychology guru to put his disappointment and his long absence together and come up with avoidance. "Maybe you'll find the answers you need as you clean out the house."

He snorted. "I'm not looking for answers."

"I'm going to pray you'll find family and God again." She said it with the absolute conviction that grew out of having received God's answers time and again.

He looked at her with all the interest of having heard something spoken in a foreign language. "Would you like to start picking out the items you want?"

She glanced at the old red clock above the stove. "I have to go. Besides, I think you should sort out what's important to you first. How would it be if I come back tomorrow and see what you've uncovered?"

"Sounds like a plan." He held the door open for her.

As she went out the back gate and along the alley to her home next door, she thought about Ace's steadfast refusal to believe Aunt Millie cared about him.

God, it seems You've sent him here to find answers he doesn't even know he wants. If so, help him find them and find love at the same time—Your love.

two

Nicole paused outside Aunt Millie's door to give herself a mental shake before she knocked. Sure, she was excited, but only because she wanted to get her hands on those antiques as soon as possible. Busloads of tourists were arriving daily. She couldn't afford to miss any sales. At the rate she was saving money, Gram would never get her cataracts removed.

It was *not* because she looked forward to seeing Ace again. She had to get it through her mind Ace was not Andrew, her friend of the past.

"It's open," Ace called.

Inside, he sat at the table, wearing a once-white T-shirt smudged with every shade of gray and black. He leaned back in his chair, crumbs and an empty coffee cup in front of him. Muddy sweat tracks trailed along his jaw. His mouth drew to a tight line. He looked hot, dirty, and discouraged.

Nicole's urgency over the antiques ground to a halt. Her heart went out to him. Perhaps it had finally hit him how much he'd missed. "Tough day?"

"Hot day. And dusty." He tipped his head from side to side as if easing a sore neck.

"Get lots done?" She'd noticed boxes filling the Dumpster. She hoped he hadn't thrown antiques out with the junk.

"Lots of nothing. I'm convinced Aunt Millie was a pack rat." He groaned as he stretched his neck.

"Sounds like you need some cheering up."

"What I need is a forklift to clean out this house."

"Would you settle for a fresh cup of coffee?"

"Just what I need. But I'll do it." He sprang to his feet, refilled the coffeepot, and turned it on.

They waited as the dark liquid dripped through, the aroma drowning out the dusty smell she'd noticed as she stepped into the house.

"You take cream or sugar?" he asked, pouring out two cupfuls when it finished.

"Milk, if you have it."

"I haven't, but I think I remember seeing some whitener." He opened the yellowed and chipped cupboards until he located the jar, screwed off the lid, and smelled the contents. "I don't know. It's probably a century old. But, hey, does a nonfood item perish?" He tipped the jar toward her.

When she saw the lumpy contents, she shuddered. "I suddenly feel like having it black."

"Wise choice."

He seemed lost in contemplation of the bubbles on his coffee as they sat across from each other.

She sipped her black coffee, her mouth protesting at the bitter taste.

"Ace?" But how could she tell him how desperately she needed to steal away his aunt's possessions when it looked as if it had finally hit home these things were all that remained of her life? Bits and pieces of a long life he could have shared if things had turned out differently.

He quirked an eyebrow. "What were you going to ask?"

She studied the contents of her cup. "Nothing."

"Hey, this is old Ace, remember? You told me all your secrets when we were young." He winked. "I haven't forgotten."

"Neither have I." He was flirting. But too many days and years had passed for her to react as if they were old friends. He was Ace, a stranger.

And yet not quite that either.

"You were the first girl who showed an interest in me." Her cheeks grew warm under his scrutiny. "I believe I was half in love with you back then." His deep chuckle bubbled down her spine.

"We were kids," she protested.

"Yeah." His teasing expression fled. "Kids. Too young and innocent to realize what lay ahead."

"I'm sorry. I know life hasn't been easy for you."

He shrugged.

She rushed on, anxious to use this opportunity. "But you're wrong about Aunt Millie."

He raised both eyebrows. "You mean she wasn't a pack rat?"

She giggled. "That part is true, but I mean she didn't forget about you."

"How comforting." His eyes glinted.

"Ace, I've been thinking about it. And it seems to me something happened. Something to explain why she didn't come for you."

His eyes had the glazed sheen of the pottery she'd bought at the art fair in Great Falls.

"Think," she urged. "There has to be some explanation."

"You mean like she lost my address and phone number and didn't realize she could get them from social services. Or maybe—" He snapped his fingers. "I know. Maybe she developed a case of selective amnesia. I'll bet that's it. Why didn't I think of it before?"

She scowled. "You're making fun of me."

"Sorry."

"Yeah, you sound sorry."

"Maybe you should accept that everything doesn't work out all neat and tidy just because it would fit nicely into your philosophy of families are forever."

She jerked to her feet, stung by his mocking tone. Planting her hands on the tabletop, she leaned over to glare at him. "Andrew Conners, we will find an explanation for why she didn't come for you."

He didn't edge back. Not a flicker of emotion in his eyes. In fact, she sensed that all feeling had been successfully quelled and only a hard, empty shell remained.

She sank back in her chair. "I believe God has brought you here for that very reason. So you can understand and open your heart to love."

He rolled his eyes toward the ceiling. "And all the time I thought I'd come to clean out my aunt's house. How could I be so mistaken?"

❧

Ace resisted the urge to rub the back of his neck. He didn't want Nicole to know how much her words affected him. He'd like to believe as she did, but it would take a miracle to convince him Aunt Millie loved him. Because if she had, why didn't she pluck him from those harsh homes? Homes where he'd been treated like free labor or where everything that mattered to him mysteriously disappeared or was denied him. But he could tell Nicole believed in miracles. She'd find out soon enough that only a few qualified for one.

If it weren't for the antiques spread out in the other room, he'd tell her to go home and mind her own business.

Okay, maybe something about her pulled at him. It was

true he'd been half in love with her back then. Not as a man-woman thing—they'd been too young for that—but there'd been a sense of connection he'd never experienced before. And never again.

"I've picked out a few things you might be interested in." He led the way to the dining room where items he'd found during the day covered the big walnut table. Picking them out for Nicole had caused his thoughts to center on her way too much. How was he going to do this job and get out without any emotional stuff if he thought of her every minute of the day?

She rushed to the table and picked up the small brass elephant. "Wonderful. I haven't seen this for years." Her face glowed. "It's what I was telling you about. Where did you find it?"

"In a desk drawer among some old papers."

A tiny frown creased her forehead. "There were three of them."

"Maybe the others will turn up." When her forehead smoothed and her smile returned, the tension in his neck eased. He shook his head feeling suddenly as if they were kids again when he couldn't bear to see her unhappy. He'd gone out of his way to make her laugh then, even though they spent considerable time in serious discussion about things that mattered to kids. But he didn't want to go back to that time of his life. He wasn't the same person he was then.

She circled the table, her eyes measuring, lighting with pleasure. She wore a simple pale green dress. It made her look slender and vibrant as an olive branch. She picked up the items and examined them carefully. When she finished, she stood in front of him. "I'll have to start a list. Wouldn't want to cheat you."

"Or yourself."

Their gazes caught and held. He could sense her jolt as if she were seeing him in a new light. No longer the Andrew of her childhood, but Ace, a man, and she, a woman. Awareness flickered across her eyes, even as it stirred his own feelings. It was more than a physical thing. It was emotional. He felt safe with her. Just like when they were children. He knew he could tell her all his secrets and she would understand. The moment tingled with the promise of discovery. Yet a chasm as big as the Atlantic Ocean separated them. She had her dreams. He had his reality.

She looked away first.

He drew in a sharp breath. They were no longer children. He had no secrets he wanted to share. Life meant simply doing his job and doing it well. Then on to the next challenge.

She looked as if she wanted to say something. Knowing her directness, figuring she'd been as aware of the electricity between them as he, he decided to stop things before they got complicated.

"You can look after the details of pricing and all that."

She jerked back and stared at the table as if something was wrong.

"Yes?" he said.

She flashed the palms of her hands upward.

"What's the problem?"

"I hate to say this, but I hoped you'd have more stuff ready to go."

"Hah. When was the last time you looked in Aunt Millie's cupboards? She has everything mixed together like some sort of conglomerate. I don't dare dump anything without sorting through it piece by piece. Why, I found the deed to the house in a cupboard along with bits of string, unmatched gloves—with holes in them, no less—and some ratty old rags. It's pathetic. That's what it is."

"Whoa. Slow down." Nicole touched his arm to still his outburst.

Unexpected unfamiliar warmth leapt along his nerves.

"I'm sorry," she murmured. "I didn't mean to put on any pressure. It's just—"

When she seemed disinclined to finish, he said, "It's just what?"

She blinked at his impatience. "Really, it's none of your concern."

He growled. "Tell me."

She gave in with a little smile. "Oh, all right, if you insist. I need the money I'd get from selling these things."

He studied the worried expression she tried to hide beneath her tight smile. "How bad do you need this money?"

"It's nothing like that. My business is sound."

"So then what's your problem?"

She sighed. "It's not really a problem. I just have to generate more income to meet some family needs. I could make a tidy profit from selling these antiques." She paused to chew her lip. "Our busy season is about to start. Tourist buses and visitors, you know."

"I didn't realize there was an urgency. At least not on your part."

She grabbed his arm, rekindling warmth along his nerves. "Maybe I could help you." Her face turned up to him with a sweet, generous expression on her lips.

If only she didn't remind him of his past. A time when he'd allowed himself, under her intense concern, to admit how much he'd longed for things that couldn't be. When he'd felt

so fiercely protective of her as she confessed her pain at her
father's death and her excitement that her mother was going
to marry again and make her dreams of family come true.

He ground the palm of his hand against his forehead. He
had no intention of getting tangled up in an emotional mess
that would leave him regretting this trip to Reliance.

No, he was going to dispose of all the memories of his aunt
and leave town as fast as he could. Yet he couldn't resist her
offer. If only to help him finish the job sooner. "Sounds like
a plan."

❧

Next afternoon Ace wiped his arm across his brow. The heat
in the house was unbearable, the job more difficult than he
could have imagined. In and out with as few complications
as possible had been his intention. Discovering the heaps of
boxes and junk shot that theory in the foot. And running into
Nicole again—seemed all she had to do was open her eyes
wide to draw him almost into her soul, make him want to
belong. But he'd stopped being a kid with childish yearnings.
He'd become a man, capable of doing a job without getting
emotionally involved. A secret weapon he'd learned to use to
his advantage.

He carried a stack of boxes outside and deposited them on
the back lawn. He lifted his head, letting the breeze cool his
skin, then folded back the flaps of another box.

"How are you getting along over there?" At the voice to his
right he looked up.

An old woman sat in an ancient rocker in the shade of the
house, watching him. Nicole's grandmother. Older, grayer
than he remembered. But what did he expect? Time took its
toll on everything and everyone.

The old woman smiled. Still the same gentle, kind, welcoming smile of his memories.

He lifted his hand in greeting. "Just great."

"It's quite a task, this sorting out Millie's belongings." Gram struggled to her feet, groaning softly as she straightened. She limped to the board fence separating the two yards and leaned against the top. "Find anything useful or interesting?"

"Not much. Mainly old newspapers and worn-out clothes. I can't imagine why Aunt Millie didn't dispose of most of this junk ages ago."

"Millie liked to keep things. She always planned to do something with it."

"What did she plan to do with these?" He pulled out a nested stack of empty egg crates.

Gram laughed, a low gentle sound in the back of her throat. "I bet she planned to recycle them but never got around to it."

"What would you do with old clothes?" He held up a dress so worn the colors had faded into streaks.

"Rag rugs. Worth a fortune at a store like Nicole's. You ought to see what she has there."

"Her store must be crammed full of treasures." Imagine. More junk like he'd been uncovering all day. Though the idea of visiting Nicole at her store held a lot of appeal. With each new box he opened, every shelf he cleaned off, he thought of Nicole—her quick smile, her intense look. Not often life surprised him, but finding Nicole still here and once again experiencing a connection had been unexpected enough to put him a hair off balance. Momentarily. And he'd ended up telling more about himself and his past than he liked to tell anyone. But it wouldn't happen again.

Returning to the older woman's comment about Nicole's

store, he said, "I'll have to drop in sometime."

"You do that, young man. My Nicole has done a wonderful job with it."

He grinned at her. " 'Course you wouldn't be the least bit prejudiced, would you?"

"I'm totally prejudiced when it comes to my granddaughters. That one in particular. She's more than a little special." She stared hard at him. "I imagine you noticed it, too."

He raised his eyebrows, saving himself the need of indicating yes or no, but he admired her directness. He shuffled through the remaining contents of the box and, finding nothing but old newspapers, carried the whole lot to the Dumpster.

Gram watched and waited as he returned and opened the next box. "It's a bit like dismantling her life, isn't it?"

Ace kept his eyes on his task as her words struck home. She'd nailed the feelings he'd struggled with all day. He felt like an intruder poking rudely through someone's life.

"I've never seen so much stuff." Going from foster home to foster home taught him not to become attached to things. More times than not, the foster family laid claim to anything he cared about.

And now lean living proved useful in his job. He could pack up everything he owned and be ready to move in minutes.

"This must be really difficult for you. Seeing so many bits and pieces of her life like this."

He shrugged, not caring to delve into it any further.

Nicole's grandmother ignored his hint. "Maybe Millie hoarded stuff because she could never forget she started with so little. In some ways she ended up the same—a houseful of belongings but alone except for a few close friends." She paused. "You were all the family she had left."

"Uh-huh." She didn't need to say anything more. He heard the accusation in her voice demanding to know why he hadn't been there for Aunt Millie. He wanted to tell her the truth; Aunt Millie hadn't been there for him. But what purpose would it serve except to add to the old woman's pain? Besides, he didn't want to talk about it.

He spoke without looking up. "I hadn't seen her in years."

"Why is that?"

He kept his attention on the contents of the box—more junk—and ignored the sharp, censorious tone of her voice.

"We lost contact."

"Didn't you want to keep in touch? You know, give her a phone call or send a Christmas card?"

What he wanted and what life offered were so far apart they didn't belong in the same world. "After a while you get used to being alone and don't think about how things might be different."

"So you're saying you wish they could have been different?"

He sneaked a look at her without turning his head. But her expression revealed only kindliness. Why was she being so persistent? Nicole and her grandmother both seemed bent on trying to change things. Or perhaps recapturing the past. But he didn't want to think about the past. It had no part of his present. His present consisted of short-term relationships that ended as soon as he moved on to a new job. It was the way he wanted it to be. "I'm happy with the status quo."

"I see."

Did he detect a note of disappointment in her voice? But what difference did it make to her?

He pushed the box aside—nothing but more junk—and attacked another box.

"I'd better go peel some potatoes for supper." But she didn't move.

Ace finally looked up to see why she lingered, mystified by the look on her face. As if she wanted something from him.

"Have a good evening," he said, not knowing what else she could want except a polite good-bye.

"Why don't you join us for supper? Say about six thirty?"

Ace hesitated. He didn't want to be a spectator at a sweet little family scene. Seeing the three of them all cozy and sure of where they belonged would only make him feel more isolated than sitting alone at Aunt Millie's table. But hungry and tired of his meager selection, he agreed. "Thanks. I'll be there."

She nodded, turned slowly, and made her way back to the house.

Ace sighed. No doubt she missed Millie. Friends for so many years. He pulled out more old clothes and tossed them into an empty box. Nothing even remotely useful. He picked up a faded chenille article. An old, threadbare housecoat unfolded across his knees, and a wave of memories engulfed him. The scent he'd been trying to ignore all day wafted over him—the flowery soap Aunt Millie used.

A boy of twelve. Too old for bedtime stories. But Aunt Millie didn't seem to realize it. So every evening during that long-ago Christmas season, he'd leaned against her shoulder, pressed his face into the chenille texture of this housecoat, breathed in the sweetness of her soap, inhaled the comfort of the routine, the security of her love—all things his alcoholic mother failed to provide. The fulfillment of his dreams and hopes.

He bundled the rag into a ball and threw it across the yard. It disappeared into the open Dumpster.

three

Nicole hurried home. "Sorry to be late." She'd spent more time at the store than she realized, anxious to make room for items from Aunt Millie's house.

"Just in time, dear." Gram stood at the stove stirring a pan of gravy. "I've invited Ace to have supper with us."

Carrie and Nicole stared at her.

"You did?" Carrie's voice squeaked. "I wish you'd told me sooner." She rushed to the tiny mirror at the end of the cupboards and wailed at her reflection. "My hair." She raced from the room, and her footsteps thundered up the stairs.

Nicole sneaked a glance in the mirror as she passed and flicked her fingers through her hair to fluff it. The bright yellow sundress she'd worn to work would have to do. She would not go clattering up the stairs like teenage Carrie.

Gram turned back to the stove. "We need to make him feel welcome. Aunt Millie would be hurt if we didn't do all we could to help him."

As Gram talked, Nicole glanced around the kitchen. The white cupboards with red trim needed to be updated. The table where they took their meals, equally out-of-date—something Gram owned since Nicole could remember. The place felt homey and comfortable to Nicole, but perhaps Ace would fail to see beyond the surface of old and worn.

"Besides," Gram continued, "when I spoke to him a little while ago, he looked tired and discouraged."

Gram's words brought Nicole full circle to her vow to discover what had gone wrong. "Gram, why didn't Aunt Millie—"

A knock interrupted her question.

"It's Ace." Carrie dashed into the room and raced for the door. She grabbed his arm and practically dragged him to a chair. Nicole spared him a glance. Freshly showered, freshly shaved, his wet hair dark. A cotton short-sleeved shirt in soft blue. A pair of navy rugby shorts. She could smell his soap and aftershave. A masculine scent as foreign in this house as new chairs would have been.

"Do you want coffee or something?" Carrie asked.

"Coffee sounds good." Ace settled into the chair, a bemused expression on his face.

Gram held a full cup toward the younger girl who carried it carefully to Ace. "Bet you're sick of cleaning out that old house."

Ace grinned. "I've thought of a few things I'd sooner be doing." He raised his gaze to Nicole and directed his question to her. "How did you spend your day?"

She poured herself a cup of coffee. Why should he care? But then who said he did? He was only making polite conversation. No need for her to turn it into anything else. "I'm making room to display Aunt Millie's things."

"You should see all the stuff Nicole has in the store," Carrie said, throwing her arms in a dramatic sweep. "Paintings and pottery and"—she turned to Nicole—"what did you call that other stuff?"

"You mean the fabric art?" Nicole studied Ace as she answered Carrie. If he showed the least annoyance with Carrie's turbo-charged enthusiasm, she would throw him bodily from the house, but he smiled at the younger girl.

She bit her lip to keep from telling her sister to stop looking so starstruck.

"That's it. Fabric art." Carrie leaned closer to Ace. "They're pictures but not paintings. More like—like—sculpting on a flat surface." She settled back, satisfied with her description. But only for a minute. "It's wonderful stuff. You should go see it."

"Must be quite a store. I'd like to see it sometime." His hazel eyes held surprising warmth and made Nicole remember how they'd shared dreams as kids. Before they'd both changed. Now all she wanted from him was Millie's antiques—and a chance to prove Aunt Millie wasn't the selfish, hard-hearted person he made her out to be. His aunt had been a sweet woman who baked casseroles for the sick right up until she was so crippled she had to have help herself. And for Nicole's high school graduation, Aunt Millie had crocheted a gossamer shawl Nicole cherished. Knowing how much pain it must have brought to the older woman's gnarled fingers to make such a delicate item, Nicole had used it only twice—for a friend's wedding and Aunt Millie's funeral.

Maybe God intended to use her family as a means of bringing Ace back to God and revealing the truth about Aunt Millie at the same time.

Gram spoke, pulling Nicole's attention back to the family dinner. "I told him what a fine job you've done on the store. Of course we were really discussing rag rugs."

Nicole's thoughts swirled. "Rag rugs?"

The amused sparkle in Ace's eyes made it impossible for Nicole to think straight. "Your grandmother told me how valuable all those old clothes of Aunt Millie's are if they're converted into rag rugs."

"That's right." She welcomed something concrete to discuss. "Didn't Aunt Millie make several?"

"I believe she did," Gram said. "Quite a few years ago. I'm surprised you remember, dear."

"I'm beginning to think Nicole doesn't forget very much." Ace's gaze held Nicole's.

She knew he referred to her memory of his confessions when they were so young.

"I believe everything is ready," Gram announced, pouring creamed peas into a bowl.

Nicole took the peas. "You sit down, Gram. I'll do that." She dished the mashed potatoes into a bowl, her movements stiff and unnatural as she felt Ace watching her.

She turned with the bowl and almost jammed it into his stomach. "Oh, I'm sorry." She hadn't heard him move across the room to stand behind her.

"Let me help." His lean fingers brushed against her hands.

She all but dropped the bowl into his grasp and spun around to pour the gravy into a server. This crackling awareness of him was totally senseless. She didn't want his presence to mean anything; yet her nerves quivered like wires taut with frost. She pulled the plate of sliced roast from the oven and hurried to the table, finding the only empty chair put her across from Ace. She took her place, pointedly looking everywhere but at the man facing her.

"Let us return thanks," Gram said.

She glanced at him then, wondering what he thought of their practice. His expression sober, he met her eyes briefly before he bowed his head. Foolishly she'd hoped he would show some amusement at Gram's lifelong habit. It would give her a reason to be angry with him. Instead she was left staring at the top of his head before she followed his example and bowed over her plate.

"Amen," Gram concluded. She picked up the tray of meat and offered it to Ace. "Help yourself." Gram waited until the food passed from hand to hand then said, "Ace, tell us about your work."

Nicole focused her attention on her plate, the salt and pepper in the center of the table, Carrie's excited expression—anywhere but Ace. His size overpowered the room. And his maleness. They didn't often share mealtimes with a man. Unless you counted the preacher. And she didn't. He was old and worn and comfortable like an old quilt.

Ace was hardly old. And comfortable? Anything but. His presence invaded her senses like a pounding rain.

Don't look. He's just a person sharing a meal. But her eyes developed a mind of their own and kept returning to his face. When his gaze touched hers, her throat tightened so she couldn't swallow.

Don't be so juvenile. You're acting like you've never before seen a man looking in your direction. With supreme effort she tore her gaze away and doused her mound of potatoes with gravy.

"I contract to a number of oil companies," he said, his expression bland.

It took a moment for Nicole to realize he'd answered Gram's question about his work.

"Mostly my job involves traveling around negotiating land deals. Helping nationals and oil companies find a middle ground."

"I heard you were a negotiator," Carrie said. "Like really scary stuff. It must be so exciting."

Ace chuckled. "Mostly I think of it as a job."

"It sounds really, really awesome. I want to know all about it," the younger girl persisted. "What was the scariest thing you ever did?"

"Can't say offhand."

"But there must be something."

"Carrie," Nicole warned.

"No. It's okay. I just have to think a minute." Ace paused. "I'd have to say the most tense situation was either when I helped with the oil well fires in Kuwait or negotiated a hostage-taking situation in Brazil."

"How exciting." Carrie's eyes shone with admiration.

"Sounds risky," Gram said.

Ace shrugged. "Just my job."

Nicole's thoughts froze. She kept her gaze on her plate. Risks? Just part of a job? As if life had no meaning. As if it didn't matter who might be worried about him. Of course, pretending you didn't have family or they didn't care would ease any concern in that direction.

But how could he have forgotten Aunt Millie? Although maybe it was a good thing she didn't know what he was up to. Imagine how she would have worried. She would have spent twice as much time praying for him.

"You must have seen the whole world," Carrie said, her voice full of awe.

"Guess I've seen most of it all right."

"I wish my life wasn't so dull. But someday I'm going to do something really, really exciting." Carrie twirled her fork in the air.

A knot squeezed the back of Nicole's neck. "Carrie, don't be thinking about throwing away your life in search of excitement."

The younger girl looked stricken. "What's wrong with a little"—she waved her arm—"variety?"

"Nicole didn't mean any harm," Gram said. "She's always been a little cautious." Her kindly smile told Nicole she understood.

Nicole nodded, grateful for Gram's defense. "I've learned not to take risks. Too many people get hurt."

"People get hurt doing perfectly normal things," Carrie insisted. "Or they're busy minding their own business and someone else does something stupid."

Nicole knew she referred to the accident that took their parents.

"Seems to me," Carrie insisted with a little pout, "you might as well have a little fun while you're here."

"There's a difference between normal risks and doing something so thoughtless and risky it's bound to hurt someone." Nicole spoke slowly, even though her stomach burned to prove the point. "But I'm sure Ace doesn't want to listen to us argue."

Carrie instantly looked contrite. "I'm sorry. You're right. Besides, I'd sooner hear about his adventures. Tell us about the fires, Ace."

Nicole met his gaze briefly. "Yes, do." As he told of his experiences it grew clear he was everything she despised—a risk taker, delighting in adventure, someone who formed no emotional ties with anyone.

After the meal, she shooed Gram into the living room. Carrie hurried out to a babysitting job. Only Ace and Nicole remained in the kitchen. She wanted him to go. They'd done the neighborly thing. And now she wanted him out of her house. Out of her life before—

He gathered up a handful of dirty cutlery and carried it to the sink. "Why don't I help you clean up?"

"You don't need to do that."

"My pleasure."

She ran hot water and washed the dishes. He pulled the towel off the rack and dried them, the silence between them brittle and uneasy.

He nudged her with his shoulder and leaned close. "You have a nice family."

She relaxed; she could talk about her family anytime. "They're unique. But in a good way."

"You're very proud of them."

"I am." She smiled, trailing her fingertip through the soapsuds.

"You know"—his eyes darkened—"I think I envy you."

"I'm fortunate to have Gram and Carrie."

"Yes, you are. That isn't what I meant, though."

She sensed him struggling to find the words he wanted.

"I remember," he began slowly, "when we were kids and you talked about how excited you were to be getting a new father. I've forgotten a lot of it, but the one thing I do recall is how fiercely you wanted to be a whole family. And now, despite losing your parents, you're still a family unit. You got your dreams."

Sadness drifted through her like a whiff of smoke. She did have what she wanted. She thanked God for it every day. And she felt sorry for anyone who didn't enjoy the same thing. What harm would it do to be generous to the poor man who'd lost the last member of his family?

"Ace, I wish things had worked out for you. I'm still sure there's an explanation for why Aunt Millie didn't take you into her home. In fact, I was about to ask Gram about it when you came for supper. Why don't we do it together?"

The look on his face shifted through a range of emotions. She tried to read them. Fear? Hope? Then blank. As if he didn't care. But she'd seen enough to believe he needed assurance he hadn't been simply pushed aside and forgotten.

"Come on." She grabbed his arm and turned him toward the living room before he could refuse. Convinced he needed to feel the warmth of a family unit, wanting him to understand what it meant, she sat beside him on the couch. She kept thinking of the young boy who wanted so much to move in with his aunt Millie.

"Gram," she began, as the older woman glanced up. "Maybe you can help us."

Gram nodded slowly, as she looked from one to the other. "I'll do my best."

"Do you remember the Christmas Ace spent with Aunt Millie about eighteen years ago?"

"I recall it well." Her voice seemed cautious.

"Wasn't there talk about Ace and his mother moving in with Aunt Millie?"

"It was discussed."

"Well, why didn't it happen? Ace seems to think Aunt Millie couldn't be bothered with a teenager, but I'm certain there has to be some reasonable explanation. What do you know about it?"

Gram pushed the stitches to the back of the knitting needle and carefully wound the yarn into a tight ball. "Aunt Millie did intend to get you, Ace. Even after your mother died." She leaned closer to study him carefully. "She had her heart set on it."

Ace pushed back against the cushions, stiffening in silent disagreement.

Before he could speak, Gram sighed and continued. "Millie never would tell me exactly what happened. She kept saying what use is an old woman to anyone anyway. He's better off with younger people. Only I know she didn't believe it. The life sort of went out of her for a while. She never seemed to be as spunky after that." She again leaned over to stare into Ace's face. "Young man, I always wondered why you didn't come see her. She pined for you to her dying day."

A shudder tiptoed along Ace's arm, tingling against Nicole's skin where their elbows touched. *Do something, say something to ease his distress.* But before she could think of what to say, his muscles tightened and steel came to his voice. "I already told Nicole I tried to contact her. After a while you accept the obvious and quit trying to bang down cement walls with your head."

Gram shook her head. *"Tsk,* boy. You've grown into a fine specimen. Millie would be busting her buttons over you. But you need to develop some sense, as well. It wasn't Millie's reluctance to have you that got in the way. It was something else. I wondered if perhaps she ran into some rather obstinate authorities. For sure she wasn't young and was already crippled up with the arthritis." Gram picked up her knitting needles. "She was a prideful woman. She didn't want to bother people with her troubles. Wouldn't even confide in me, and after all we'd been through together. Best friends for all those years."

Ace jerked to his feet. "Thanks for the tasty meal."

"You're welcome, boy. Come again anytime."

Nicole followed him to the door. "Sorry it wasn't much help."

"Didn't expect it to be. I'm no longer bothered by the whole business." He grinned, driving the fierceness from his expression. "So don't you be bothering your pretty little head about it."

"I'm only looking for an answer."

"I know. You want everything to turn out nice and neat like your dreams. You want to defend your belief in forever families. All that sort of stuff."

He made her sound like an idealistic idiot. She opened her mouth to protest, but he grabbed her hand and pulled her outdoors.

"Are you coming to look at what I found today?"

"You think you can make me forget about defending Aunt Millie by dragging me over to look at her things?"

He screwed up one side of his face. "Nope. Don't think that would work." He pulled her down a step. "Maybe if we stand under that leafy maple tree and enjoy the evening, you'd forget."

Her cheeks warmed. He was flirting again. Or did the words fall out of his mouth without thought? Yet how long had it been since she'd known the pleasure of a man's company? Longer than she cared to remember. But now was not the time. Or the place.

And certainly not the man.

"I turned down a date so I could rescue Aunt Millie's antiques from being ignominiously relocated to the Dumpster, so let's go see what you've found." She pulled her hand away and tucked it safely against her side.

"Really? You turned down a hot date for me? I'm flattered."

"It wasn't all that hot. Just a schoolteacher friend who is going away for summer school."

"Man or woman friend?"

"A very nice woman." She could smell his aftershave. An exotic mixture of sea breezes and foreign spices.

"I suppose you have a long queue of admirers?"

Her mind slipped away to places fed by the scent—foreign, exciting shores with unfamiliar vegetation and the cry of strange birds.

"Still counting?" His deep voice shivered through her brain, becoming part of the jungle beat of her imagination.

"Huh?"

"I was wondering how many admirers."

She brought her thoughts back to Reliance, Montana.

Did he want to know if she had a romantic interest? "Seems to me there's no one here but you." Mentally she smacked her palm against her forehead. *Good move, Nicole. Bound to convince him you aren't interested in him. Yeah. Right.*

❧

He chuckled. From her pink cheeks and the way her gaze darted away from his, he guessed she'd flirted with him against her better judgment. He didn't want her to stop. "Just you and me. I think I might like that." In fact he flirted right back. What was the matter with him? He didn't want her to get the wrong idea. He was a loner. And she was family with a capital *F* bent on trying to make him believe in something similar.

He didn't want anything to do with it.

"Did you get some more sorting done in the house?" she asked.

Now would be the time to run as fast as he could in the opposite direction. Instead, he reached for her hand and led her through the back gate toward Aunt Millie's house. "Come and see." Was that hoarseness his voice?

As he reached around to open the door, she pulled away. He let his hand drift toward his side. Good thing one of them had some sense. But as he leaned close to turn the knob, his arm brushed her shoulder. He looked at her with more interest than he knew was wise in view of his decision to be in and out of this job without getting involved emotionally.

Her hair glistened in the slanting evening rays, trapping diamonds of gold and silver in the dark strands. She smelled like warm summer days and honey.

For one heartbeat he wondered what it would be like to be part of her world, and then he shoved aside the idea, pushed the door open, and followed her inside.

The heavy, hot air in the room crowded him. Pressed his foolish interest into deep crevices in his heart. He'd seen weird chemical reactions between rocks and acids in labs across the world—smoke, crackling noises, or a kaleidoscope of changing colors. Almost defying logic. But they were nothing compared to the chemistry pluming through him.

"Where are they?" she asked.

Reality check. Ignore the electricity crackling through the air. We're here to talk about antiques. He nodded toward the dining room and stuffed his fingers into his back pockets as she hurried through the door. He followed more slowly.

She'd have to be dead not to feel the attraction between them. Obviously she did and was uncomfortable with it. Which would explain her haste to escape to the other room.

The table was crowded with stuff he'd added since yesterday. The floor held its share, too, but she only glanced at the collection.

"Ace, I was sure Aunt Millie would have confided in Gram

and told her what happened." Her dark eyes met his, and his heart kicked hard at the concern in them.

He sighed deeply. Would they ever get past this Aunt Millie thing? "Nicole, it really doesn't matter. I accepted the whole business a long time ago. I've learned to live with it. Fact is, I never think about it unless someone brings it up."

Her eyes flickered. Or perhaps only the light through the west window caught in them. "I think it matters."

"How so?"

"I think it's made you afraid of getting close to people."

"Who says I'm afraid?" He closed the distance between them. If she wanted proof to the contrary, he could provide it here and now. He brushed the back of his fingers along her cheek.

He shouldn't have done it.

The jolt that burned down his arm went straight to his heart, threatening locks on doors he didn't intend to open. The look in her eyes—intense, uncertain—twisted like a suddenly discovered key.

Forget the locks.

Forget the promises he'd made and kept these past dozen or more years.

Only one thing mattered: He wanted her in his arms.

He reached for her, but she stepped away, suddenly very interested in the framed sampler he'd leaned against the wall.

"Would you look at this? It's dated 1908. Aunt Millie's mother must have done it." She picked it up and held it to the light. "It's exquisite."

Her gaze slid past him.

His breath stuck in his throat.

"You'll be keeping it, of course. It's a family heirloom."

He had no family, didn't believe in it, and didn't want to go over the subject again.

She looked past him to the living room where he'd stacked boxes.

"Wow. You still have a lot of work ahead."

"I don't think there's any end to it. I'm sure they're multiplying. You don't suppose boxes breed like mice?"

She giggled, and he congratulated himself on erasing the tension from her shoulders.

"I can't imagine what's in all of them," she said. "I mean. . . one old lady. What would she have accumulated if she'd had a dozen kids?"

"You mean besides a gigantic headache?"

She grinned then glanced at the outer door.

He grasped at a reason to make her stay. "You want to open a couple and see if you unearth any treasures? Though I warn you I've spent all day at this, and what you see"—he waved at the items he'd carried to the dining room—"is the extent of my findings."

"And some very nice finds, too." But she crossed the room and knelt beside a large box. "Sure you don't mind?"

Mind? Could a man mind leaning against a wall watching a pretty girl sneeze as dust tickled her nose? Not likely. "Go ahead."

"It looks like letters and cards."

"I'll get a garbage bag." He returned and sat on the floor, close enough to breathe in her sweet scent. "Dump them in here."

"But don't you want to check and see what they are?" She pulled some yellowed, lined paper from an envelope.

"Probably from long dead relatives I never heard of." But if it kept Nicole at his side reading every word, he wasn't about to complain, and he grabbed a handful of letters and cards and skimmed through them.

After a half hour she sighed and tilted her head back. "I suppose these could be sorted in some fashion. Perhaps they'd make good research material."

He laughed. "Good try, but admit it. It's nothing but junk. Should have been burned four hundred years ago."

She giggled. "Maybe fifty years ago." She dug in and retrieved a box tied with grocery-store string. "Wait—look at this." She turned the box toward him. *ANDREW* was printed on the bottom in large letters.

"You better open it."

He shook his head. "She's only reused a box with my name on it. It doesn't mean a thing." But for one fraction of a second he'd hoped it did. When would he truly stop yearning for something more? "You go ahead."

Her gaze held his another heartbeat, and then she bowed over the box, broke the string, and lifted the lid. On the very top sat a chipped, faded ornament made of plaster of Paris.

His lungs wouldn't work. His eyes hurt. He stared at the cheap figure of a collie dog every bit as ugly as the day he bought it. Why had Aunt Millie kept it all these years?

Nicole turned it bottom up. Her brow wrinkled as she read the words he knew were scratched there.

"Aunt Millie from Andrew."

Her eyes widened as she stared at him. "You gave this to her." She sounded surprised. Even a bit amazed. "How special."

❧

Nicole could feel Ace's shock but watched his rigid control return quickly and firmly to his face.

"It was just a cheap gift." He grabbed the little dog from her and ground it into his palm. "Why would she keep it?"

"Maybe because she cared."

"Sure. Just like she cared about all these old rags." He swept away a pile. "And these old letters. She probably couldn't even remember who half these people were." When he moved to throw the ornament in the garbage, she stopped him.

"Why is it so hard to think she might have cared? Does it interfere with your theories of life or something?" She shook the box in his face. "Have you seen anything else labeled with a name? Anything?"

He only glowered fiercely at her.

"Of course you haven't. Everything else was just junk, and Aunt Millie would probably be the first to admit it. This" —she rattled the box—"meant enough for her to write your name on it."

He rolled his eyes. "Yeah, right. Next you'll be telling me she prayed for me every night."

"I'm certain she did." She pulled a letter from the box and studied the address. "How strange. This has your name on it." She checked the next envelope in the stack and then the next. "This is odd. These letters are addressed to you. They've been returned."

"Uh-huh. One for every Christmas, I suppose."

She frowned at him. "You're nothing but a skeptic. Here." She shoved them toward him. "See for yourself."

Sitting back, she watched him examine several returned letters. But when he made no move to open them, she grabbed one back and carefully opened it. "Afraid you might discover the truth?"

"Just not curious." But his gaze was riveted on her fingers

as she unfolded the pages, brittle along the edges. "This one is dated years ago." She skimmed the words then slowly read them aloud.

"Dear Andrew, I have tried and tried to contact you to no avail. My letters are returned. I've been told not to phone, and when I tried, the number had been changed. Yet I will keep trying. My heart is aching. They won't let me see you or speak to you. They say it is best for you. They say it's what you want."

Nicole paused. "The words are blurred here." She gasped. "Aunt Millie must have cried as she wrote this."

Ace looked away, his face devoid of expression.

"Ace, don't you see? This proves she tried. It's like Gram said—someone wouldn't let her see you. Poor Aunt Millie."

He didn't move or acknowledge her words. Suddenly he thrust the box from her hands, letters fanning across the floor.

"It's a little late, wouldn't you say?"

four

"It's too late for you and Aunt Millie to be a family, but now you know she cared. Doesn't it make a difference?" She wanted so much for him to allow love into his life. She couldn't imagine being so alone. No ties. No family.

Her thoughts blurred, and one idea blazoned across her mind—she wanted this for her sake as much as his. She wanted him whole. Ready to embrace family and love. Somewhere, deep in her heart, lived a connection between them. Something that had begun eighteen years ago and lay dormant until now. But before they could take a step toward each other, she silently warned herself, he had to return to his faith in God. She would never allow herself to care deeply for a man who, in his own words, had put God on the back burner.

This discovery of Aunt Millie's caring, an answer to her prayer, would surely begin the healing, restoration process for him.

He took her hands, held them so hard her fingers squished together as his gaze bored into hers. "Is that what you think?" His voice rasped. "A few old letters and I'm somehow magically all right in your eyes? Will everything that went wrong in my life be erased? I'll be fixed?"

She started to nod then changed her mind and shook her head. "I don't know."

"Let's find out." He grasped her shoulders and leaned toward her, his hazel eyes intense and demanding.

He meant to kiss her. Perhaps punish her for suggesting he needed to be fixed. She didn't want a harsh kiss. Yet she couldn't deny she was curious. What was this powerful connection between them? Nostalgia or something else? She had to find out. She leaned into his embrace.

His mouth, hard at first, softened, and he drew her closer.

Nicole relaxed into his arms. It was like returning home to a warm cup of chocolate after a cold winter outing. Like finding a long-lost friend. Ace, a friend she'd been missing for eighteen years.

"Umm," he murmured against her lips. "You taste good." He edged his back against the couch and cradled her head on his shoulder. "I've thought of you over the years and wondered how you were." He chuckled, the sound rumbling beneath her ear. "If I'd known you turned out so good, I might have come sooner."

She tipped her head and studied him. The tiny pale lines around his eyes from squinting into the sun. The streaked blond highlights from the same harsh sun. The dark shadow of his whiskers. The familiar face of long ago yet grown stronger, leaner, harder. And so very masculine. As was the scent of soap and spices.

She'd only been ten when he was here, but even then she'd glimpsed the man the boy would become. Was it possible she'd fallen in love with the boy/man even then? After all, both of them held the potential of who they would become. Maybe she'd been subconsciously waiting all these years for him to return.

"I wish you'd come back a long time ago. For Aunt Millie's sake. For yours." She paused then whispered, "And mine." And she wrapped her arms around him. This was where he belonged. Back where he'd first found the love of family, the love and grace of God. He'd finally found his way back. She thanked God for the return of the prodigal.

He rubbed his chin across the top of her head. "Admit it. I was your first love."

"I'll never give you the satisfaction of confessing such a thing." She stroked the plain white button of his cotton shirt. She wouldn't let him know she felt at home with him. Not yet. Not until he discovered for himself what she already knew—this was where he belonged. The place where he'd let go of the hard Ace and return to the faith-filled, gentler Andrew.

He tipped her chin up so he could kiss her again, softly.

She pressed her palm against his cheek. She could hardly wait to see his transformation. She only hoped it would be swift. She'd already waited a very long time.

The phone jangled.

She jerked back, expecting him to answer it.

"The machine will get it," he murmured.

It clicked on. "Ace here. You know what to do."

And then a voice boomed from the speaker. "Ace? Ace, are you there? It's Bruce. Just thought I should warn you. LaRue's on the prowl again. He's looking for you. Sounded as mad as all get out."

The caller paused, and Nicole sat up straight, pushing away from Ace's embrace.

"Sorry to say the new secretary told him you were in that neck of the woods. Best keep an eye out for him. Wouldn't want to see you dead or bleeding. Call me."

Dead? Bleeding? Icy tension twisted around Nicole's spine. Her heart beat erratically and far too fast, as if she'd had too many caffeine-loaded cups of coffee. She'd heard him talk about his job, heard him describe himself as a negotiator, but it had seemed unreal, too far away to touch her world.

She scooted along the floor putting a safe distance between them. "What was that all about?" she asked.

"Just a fella from the office."

"I mean the dead and bleeding part."

He laughed like it was a joke, but she gave him a hard look, silently demanding an answer.

"It's just one of those everyday sort of eco guys. Always got his shirt in a knot about gas wells and pipelines. I deal with his kind all the time."

"Then why did this—whatever his name is from the office— think he should warn you?"

"Precaution. Nicole, it's nothing I haven't dealt with a hundred times."

His words most certainly did not make her feel better. She took a deep breath. "I don't like—"

"Risks," he finished for her. "I know. But believe me, this is only some guy looking for free media coverage."

She wanted to believe him. Believe this wasn't anything out of the ordinary. She wanted it so bad she pushed aside the alarm skidding along her veins. Besides, she did have a habit of being overly cautious, and she admitted it.

"Come here, and I'll make you forget all your worries."

Amused at the way he waggled his eyebrows, she never-theless shook her head and backed away. It was too soon. She needed to be sure of some things before she let her heart have its way. "I have to get home."

❧

Ace leaned over a box, his hands idle. He'd moved cartons

around all morning but hadn't been able to sort their contents. Thoughts of Nicole filled his mind to the point that he couldn't concentrate on anything else.

She was everything he wanted.

Everything he couldn't have.

He'd learned his lesson a long time ago. And he wasn't about to forget it.

But he could barely hear his mental arguments over the pull of his emotions. Last night as they'd said good night under the golden glow from the light over the back door, she looked like an Egyptian goddess with her inky black hair and dark eyes.

He wanted to kiss her, but she again resisted. He felt her caution. Knew he didn't measure up to her standard.

Sure, they'd shared something eighteen years ago, but it wasn't possible to recapture it. He knew it wasn't. They were as far apart as the east was from the west. Yet—if they turned and faced each other—

What about his long-held vow: Never get involved in a relationship promising forever? Forever didn't exist.

He flipped open the lid of another box and stared into the contents. More old clothes and shoes. More worn-out appliances.

What was he doing here? Did he hope to find the belonging he'd never known?

He jerked to his feet, grabbed a cup of coffee, and went outside. He needed to think. He didn't belong in Nicole's world, and for sure he didn't belong in her life. He'd never fit. Not Ace Conners. He'd never been allowed to fit, and now it was too late. He was a loner. Dreaming of belonging, a family, a home—he must be out of his mind. Hadn't life taught him enough hard lessons?

He gulped his coffee. He needed to finish emptying out Aunt Millie's house and move on before Nicole got hurt.

About to head back indoors, Ace stopped. Every muscle in his body tensed. Had someone moaned? He glanced over the fence, saw nothing but the flower-filled yard and a book lying open on Gram's rocking chair. Yet the nerves along the back of his neck tingled. A sure sign of some sort of danger. He breathed quietly through parted lips as he assessed the situation. Slowly he turned, scanning the view. Nothing. He sighed. What did he expect? Snipers in the treetops? An armed ambush? Yet he couldn't shake the feeling something was wrong.

He eased toward the fence, poised for any possibility, and tensed when he saw a body on the ground next to the flowers. Then realized it wasn't an ambush.

"Gram." The old lady lay in the pathway between her sweet peas and azaleas. He vaulted the fence and knelt at her side. "What happened? Are you hurt?"

Gram groaned. "I stepped on a rock and twisted my foot."

The foot had already swollen like a ball. Ace untied the laces and pulled off her shoe.

"I tried to call out, but I couldn't. I prayed you'd hear me." Gram's voice thinned with pain.

"Let's get you inside and put some ice on that." He lifted her, surprised at how little she weighed.

Inside, he settled her in the big armchair, found ice, and packed it in a towel around her ankle.

"Maybe I should take you to the emergency room."

Gram waved the idea away. "It's feeling better already."

"Can I get you anything? Painkillers, coffee, something to eat?"

Gram laid her head back. "I could use a cup of tea if you don't mind."

Ace hurried to the kitchen, found the kettle, and put it to boil. He located acetaminophen tablets on a shelf next to the sink and poured out two. He carried the tea in and set a cup next to Gram's elbow. She took the pills without argument.

"You are a godsend," she said after a moment. Again she put her head back and closed her eyes.

Ace sat quietly at her side, waiting for her to fall asleep, but in a few minutes she lifted her head and shuffled backward in the chair. "My granddaughter has been spending a lot of time at your house." She studied him openly, quizzically.

"She's anxious to get her shelves stocked with Aunt Millie's antiques."

"There's more to it than that, young man. I've seen the look in her eyes when she doesn't know I'm watching."

Ace grinned. So Nicole wasn't as indifferent to him as she tried to make him think. Sort of made him feel good. Then steel vibrated along his spine. *No emotional involvement. Remember?*

"So where do you go from here?" Gram asked.

Did she mean between him and Nicole? Or his job? He decided he'd stick to talking about his job. "I'm planning to negotiate some lease problems in the Arctic."

Gram fixed him with a keen gaze. "And where does Nicole figure into this?"

"She belongs here with you and Carrie, her friends, and her store."

Gram leaned forward. "I don't want to see that girl hurt."

Ace considered her a moment. "No reason she should be."

Gram studied him so carefully he felt like a small, naughty

boy. "You're a fine man, Andrew Conners. But you have to decide what it is you want."

What did he want? At one time it would have been exactly what he could have here—a family, love, and all the things that went with that. But he no longer knew if it was enough. Or maybe it was too much. He'd grown used to being alone.

And lonely.

But did he want to spend the rest of his life like that?

No. A thousand times, no.

Yet could he change?

"Is it possible to have what one wants?" he asked.

Gram nodded slowly. "If a person wants something badly enough, anything is possible. People can change. They do all the time. Sometimes without realizing it." She paused. "Andrew, how is your relationship with God?"

"God and I have lost touch."

She tsked. "That's where you need to start your journey. Get back in touch with God. Learn to believe in His love. You'll be surprised how easy it is to put the rest of your life together once you accept that."

If only things could be so simple. He knew they weren't. Wanting, needing, and getting didn't necessarily follow in logical sequence. Life had taught him not to expect miracles.

"Bring me that photo album, and I'll tell you about Nicole."

He did as she asked, settling the album across her knees and pulling a chair close so he could see the pages.

"Here she is at her high school graduation."

He studied the pictures of Nicole in a frothy red dress. He looked at poses of Nicole alone, gathered with classmates, surrounded by her parents and Carrie.

Gram tapped the book. "She was the prettiest girl there."

Ace agreed. She shone with excitement.

"Here she is getting ready to leave for university." Gram flipped a few pages. "She was always bringing friends home with her." There were pictures of Nicole with a variety of girls and boys at her side.

"Where did she go to school? What did she take? What were her plans?"

Gram laughed. "Sounds like you want to know everything."

He shrugged. He didn't intend to let the older woman guess how much he wanted to know. What made Nicole tick? Why did she cling so firmly to family? What scared her and why? What was responsible for that overdeveloped fear of risk?

"Very well. She went to the University of Montana. Started in business management then switched to history. She quit to come home when her parents died. I told her I could manage without her." Gram snorted. "But we both knew I couldn't. She always thought she'd wasted her time at university. Complains she never got a degree or anything useful from it. I remind her God knew what she needed. Her courses in business, history, and even art are exactly right to help her run the store." Gram tapped the page and seemed lost in thought. "Such a good girl. And so smart. She knew exactly what sort of business to start." She sighed and suddenly seemed to remember Ace sat at her side, fascinated with the insights Gram provided.

Nicole, intense and idealistic as a child, had grown into an idealistic young woman. She'd learned how to combine that with a wide streak of business acumen. *Way to go, Nicole.* He had no reason to be so proud of her. Just the same, he was.

"No special boyfriend?"

Gram grew thoughtful. "There was one I thought would

last. But after Nicole came home to help raise Carrie, I never saw him again. Nicole only said they had different agendas." She sighed heavily. "I don't suppose too many young men would want to be burdened with an old lady and a teenage girl."

Ace studied the pictures. "Getting a family might seem like a bonus to some." It sounded mighty attractive to him, especially when the package came tied up with Nicole. Too bad it was too late for him.

Gram closed the album, her finger holding the page. She shifted so she could study Ace.

He sensed her measuring him, trying to decide if he met her approval, if he would be good or bad for her granddaughter. He smiled, calm and in control. Perhaps she'd share the answer with him when she figured it out.

She nodded slowly. "Let me tell you about my Nicole."

Ace leaned forward slightly, his interest on full alert. He wanted to hear everything.

"Nicole is. . .well, cautious, I guess. She feels doubly responsible to make sure both Carrie and I are safe. Why, that girl, even when I said the store was hers to do with as she wanted, she was so careful. Vowed she'd never go in debt. She's careful with everything she does. I don't think she's ever gotten over losing her father and then her mother and stepfather. Not that I'm complaining. As long as Nicole is in charge, I know we don't have to worry. But that said, I don't ever want to be a burden to her. She should think about what she needs and wants in life. Not always be thinking about what she thinks we need."

Gram shook her head. "Here I am rambling on. Probably doesn't make a lick of sense to you. But be warned." She shook her finger at Ace. "I would not stand by idly if someone hurt her."

He took her hand and squeezed it gently. "I think Nicole is far more resilient than you give her credit for. Sure, she's cautious. She has a lot of responsibility. She's had to make some sacrifices. But she's smart and knows what she wants." They studied each other. Gram's expression remained stern.

Finally, Ace grinned. "Gram, I'm not some monster. I would never intentionally hurt her." But as he thought about how good it felt to kiss her last night, her initial eager response then her caution, he wondered if it was already too late. But he reminded himself she was the one who had backed away. She was the one who knew when to put on the brakes. He, Ace Conners, known for his cool detachment, had been taken momentarily off guard by something from the past that reared its head and demanded equal time. It was true he'd been half in love with her when they were both much younger. She'd offered him something he'd never known before—a sincere interest in him, his hopes and dreams. With her and her alone, he had discovered a warm place deep inside his heart. A place now atrophied beyond redemption.

"See that you don't." With a quick nod as if she'd settled the matter to her satisfaction, Gram turned back to the album and continued to point out pictures of Nicole and tell Ace stories. Nicole was everything he'd imagined: fun, sensitive, feisty.

He rose to get more tea for Gram and fetch an older photo album. They were poring over the pictures of Nicole in grade school when Carrie burst through the door.

She took one look at Gram with her ankle packed in ice and squealed. "Gram!" She skidded across the floor and fell on her knees beside the older woman. "What happened?" And burying her face in Gram's lap, she burst into tears.

"Now, now, Carrie. Hush, child. It's nothing. Just a little bruise. I'm okay. Take more than a little rock to do me real harm." She patted Carrie's head as the young girl sobbed.

"Are you sure?" Carrie managed.

"I'll be just fine. Don't you worry."

Carrie hugged Gram and kissed her neck. "I don't know what I'd do if anything happened to you."

Ace saw the glint of tears in Gram's eyes as she rubbed Carrie's back. "You run and wash your face, and then we'll talk about supper."

Gram wiped at the corner of her eyes. "My girls are both so fragile." Her eyes held a silent warning.

But he got it. He understood. *Don't hurt my girls.*

He wouldn't. He'd be in and out of Reliance before anyone noticed. Nicole would take away the old things she wanted and forget him again—just another old thing from the past.

Even before he'd completed the thought, he knew Nicole wanted more. But what? Certainly to fix his past, which couldn't be done. He could not go back. But perhaps she hoped for even more than that. Did she hope to fit him into her life? Again, not possible.

He felt a tremor of danger. Her intensity, her ideals, spoke to his long-denied dreams. Both he and Nicole stood a very real chance of getting hurt if either of them let those childish wishes get in the way.

He turned away, unwilling to let Gram see his eyes. Knowing she would see more than he cared for her to see.

five

Nicole stepped into the kitchen and stared. Gram sat in her rocking chair, her foot elevated and wrapped in icepacks. Carrie and Ace peered into a bubbling pot on the stove. Carrie held a spoon and licked her lips.

"A little more salt, maybe."

Ace nodded. "Agreed. Other than that, this is the best pot of clam chowder you could ask for."

Had she walked into the wrong house?

She savored the moment, knowing reality would erase it as soon as one of them saw her standing in the doorway.

Gram glanced up. "Nicole, don't look so surprised."

The two at the stove turned.

Carrie dropped the spoon and hurried toward her. "Gram hurt her foot. Ace found her and helped her, and now he's helping me make supper. Gram said she'd like some clam chowder, so Ace is showing me his way of making it." Carrie halted a few inches from Nicole and waved her arms. "Can you imagine him being such a good cook?"

Nicole's gaze locked with Ace's. All she could think of was last night. How good it had felt to be in his arms. To be kissed. He half winked. Was he remembering last night, too? Warmth surged up her neck. She was thankful no one but Ace paid her much attention.

His gaze remained unwaveringly on her. "I have a very limited knowledge of cooking. This is only something one of the camp cooks taught me because I requested it so often. Said if I liked it so much I might as well learn to make it." He set the lid carefully back on the pot.

Nicole hugged Carrie quickly before she hurried to Gram's side. "Tell me what happened."

Gram dismissed the whole thing with a wave. "It was nothing. A mean-natured rock thought it could get the best of me." She snorted. "Take a lot more than that to stop me."

Nicole raised her gaze to Ace. "Did she see a doctor?"

Gram flicked one hand, and Ace shook his head. "She refused. But the swelling is almost gone. However"—he gave Gram a hard look—"if it's still painful in the morning I'd suggest you push, pull, or drag her in."

Gram huffed. "There'll be no need, I tell you."

Nicole gently unwrapped the ankle. There was redness from the ice but little swelling. She touched the foot, and Gram flinched. "Tomorrow morning if it still hurts, we're off to the doctor."

"We'll see," Gram muttered.

"Thank you for coming to the rescue," Nicole said to Ace.

"No problem."

He wore the same old T-shirt he'd had on a couple of days ago and jeans with smudged patches of dirt. He'd obviously been going through dusty boxes. Had he found it annoying to have his work interrupted? She studied his expression. He didn't look upset as he handed placemats to Carrie and took a stack of soup bowls from the cupboard. In fact, he looked to be having the time of his life. It surprised her how easily he seemed to fit in.

"I'll be back as soon as I change." She slipped away to pull on white cotton shorts and a bright yellow tank top. As she skimmed a comb through her short hair she stared at herself in the mirror. Imagine coming home every day to Ace in the kitchen, Carrie and Gram happily at his side. She gently slapped one cheek. "Nicole Thomas. Give your head a shake. You and Ace are from opposite ends of the pole." Mentally she listed the reasons they could never belong together. He enjoyed the challenge of risks, downplayed them, lived happily without family. Or at least insisted he did. Most of all, he did not have a living faith.

She snorted, remembering one of Gram's acerbic comments about such people. *Good thing God didn't stop believing they existed.* She didn't know that Ace had stopped believing in God's existence, perhaps just His love and care.

Ace needed to learn to trust God again. Until he did, he was off limits to her. No more kissing. It was too tempting. She closed her eyes briefly. Even if he returned to faith, what made her think a cozy little family scene like the one downstairs was going to change who both she and Ace were? It wasn't possible. She scowled at herself for a second, trying to convince herself to stop hoping. But if he could admit Aunt Millie had loved him, if he were to stop hiding behind Ace and remember he was Andrew, if he stopped running from God. . .

She shook her head. It would take a miracle.

Her scowl fled, replaced by a wide grin. Miracles were God's business. She would pray for a miracle for Ace then sit back and watch God work.

She hurried downstairs and stopped outside the kitchen to watch.

"Why bother with forks?" Carrie insisted. "Just more to wash up."

Ace held up a spoon and then a fork. "I suppose you're right, though I never thought four tiny bits of hardware could make such a big difference in the cleanup. Wouldn't be a wee bit lazy, would you?" He waggled his eyebrows at Carrie, making her giggle.

"Just efficient," she said.

Gram smiled at the two of them. "We've spoiled Carrie."

Nicole wanted to protest but hung back watching the interaction between the other three.

Carrie bent to kiss Gram's cheek. "But look how good I turned out."

Tears sprang to Nicole's eyes. Family was meant to be like this—caring for each other despite differences in age and interests.

Ace turned and caught her dashing a tear from the corner of her eyes and smiled gently.

He fit in so well. As if he belonged right here with them. Did he ever imagine himself as part of a family? Or did his work satisfy even his deepest longings? She knew it couldn't, but he had been hurt and disappointed when Aunt Millie didn't come for him. He'd grown wary, calloused.

Yes, it would take a miracle. Hope found its way into her heart. God could reach into the most damaged, fearful soul. Ace would soon see how easy it was to belong and be loved. Dreams could come true.

"Soup's on," he said softly.

Ace helped Gram to the table, while Carrie ladled soup into each bowl. Nicole took the loaf of warm bread from the microwave, sliced it, and put it in a basket.

"Guess what I did today," Carrie said, after Gram said grace.

"Found a million bucks?" Nicole passed the bread to Ace. His finger slid along her thumb. She smiled quickly then ducked her head and concentrated on spreading butter on her slice of bread.

"Dug up buried treasure?" Gram suggested, as she tasted the soup. "This is delicious, Ace."

He tipped his head. "Thank you. From someone of your experience, I take that as a real compliment."

Carrie swept an annoyed look around the table. "You guys." To Ace she said, "They're always teasing me."

He grinned at her. "It's because they care."

"Well, sometimes they care too much." She shot Nicole another dark look, but Nicole knew she wasn't really offended. It was part of the game they played.

As if to prove her point, Carrie sprang forward on her chair. "I taught the twins to ride their bikes without their training wheels."

"Good for you. Carrie babysits the five-year-old twins across the street," Nicole explained to Ace.

Gram nodded approval.

Carrie turned to Ace. "Isn't that great?"

Ace gave Carrie a serious look. "If everyone is still in one piece."

"Yup. I probably have the most damage." She showed her bruised elbow.

Nicole glanced around the table. Such a simple meal, but the creamy chowder—full of vegetables and clams—and the yeasty warm bread satisfied in a comforting way. Good home-style food. It seemed to breathe family and togetherness. And Ace in the center. Passing food as if he belonged. Joining in the conversation as if he'd always been there. A golden glow filled Nicole. Her prayed-for miracle seemed so close.

Carrie suddenly looked at them all. "So what did everyone else do today?"

Gram's eyes twinkled as she answered. "I entertained a handsome visitor. Showed him the family photo albums."

Carrie and Nicole groaned.

"You didn't show him the one where I had my lips curled back to show my missing teeth, did you?" Carrie demanded.

Gram nodded. "Certainly I did."

Carrie wrinkled her nose then gave Nicole a mischievous look. "Did you show him the one with Nicole in that pouffy pink dress?"

Again Gram nodded.

Carrie hooted. "The Jolly Pink Pumpkin."

Nicole met Ace's gaze. He grinned widely. "I thought it was rather. . .rather. . ."

Carrie giggled. "Come on. I dare you to say what you really thought."

Her insides suddenly quivering, Nicole jerked her gaze away to stare at her soup bowl.

Ace took his time answering the question. "I just cannot think of the right word."

Carrie laughed. "I guess not."

Ace continued. "I told Gram I wish I could have been here to see it in person. Didn't I, Gram?"

"You couldn't quit looking, that's a fact."

Carrie laughed loudly. "Pretty unbelievable all right."

Nicole felt Ace's look and slowly lifted her head. At the glow in his hazel eyes, a jolt shot along her nerves. There was no mistaking his approval. He smiled slowly. "I enjoyed seeing her growing up."

Carrie sobered. "I should talk. I hate some of the pictures of me in those albums, but Gram has a fit every time I try to sneak them out."

"Family history," Gram said. "Lots of good memories in those pictures."

"Yeah." Nicole's voice was dry. "Most of the memories are from our knee-jerk reaction every time you bring them out."

Gram chuckled. "You ought to see yourselves."

Nicole looked at Carrie. "The album in the closet."

Carrie nodded. "I'll get it."

Gram pressed her hand to her chest. "Girls, you wouldn't."

But Carrie raced out of the room.

"This is a dirty trick," Gram protested. "She knows I can't chase her down."

Nicole stacked the dirty dishes and carried them to the counter. "How dignified would that be?"

Gram grunted. "Forget dignity."

Ace leaned back in his chair, watching the proceedings with a bemused look on his face.

Nicole felt she had to explain. "She has some dreaded photos, too."

"Poor Gram. What chance does she have against the two of you?"

Gram patted his hand, her face softening at his defense of her. "None whatsoever. I don't know how I put up with them." She sighed heavily. "It's been a trial as you can plainly see." The proud gleam in her eyes as she looked at Nicole dispelled any doubt about how she truly felt.

Nicole kissed the top of her head. "I love you, too, Gram."

Ace laughed.

Nicole wondered what he thought of the familiar, irreverent

way they treated each other. It probably wasn't what he thought of when he pictured an ideal family. But then what did he imagine? For Ace, it seemed family meant disappointment, broken promises, all sorts of things that didn't fit in with their open, honest love for each other.

She leaned against Gram's shoulder. How grateful she was for the stability this dear grandmother had provided through the loss of two fathers and a mother. She and Carrie were so blessed. She sent a quick thank-you prayer heavenward.

Carrie skidded back into the room, swept her arm across the table to clear a spot in front of Ace, and plunked down a frail, black photo album. She opened it in the middle and pointed. "This is Gram growing up."

The two heads bent over the pages, Carrie's bright golden one, Ace's darker, sun-streaked hair.

If only she could hold them all together just like this. For a moment she let herself dream. First, Ace would allow God's love into his life. It was her most fervent prayer. And then. . .

She pushed the thought away. Even if he did that, and she would pray earnestly he did, it didn't mean he'd want family. And even if he did, why would he want one consisting of an elderly woman and a teenage girl? He'd want his own family.

Ace finally looked up, his gaze resting on Gram. "These are beautiful photos."

Gram preened. "Thank you."

Carrie grimaced. "If you don't mind the funny clothes."

Gram sighed. "As I recall, Carrie, you were asking about our day." She turned to Ace. "I'm afraid I managed to make a mess of yours. I'm sorry, though I'm so grateful for your help."

Carrie and Nicole echoed her thanks. A shiver raced up Nicole's spine, but she refused to dwell on what might have happened if Ace hadn't heard Gram.

"An afternoon in your company was a pleasant reprieve," Ace said. "I didn't know if I could face another box of stuff. I've thought of simply dumping everything in one fell swoop, but I've found important papers and priceless antiques in with the junk, so I have to sort through it all." He smiled at Nicole. "I'm sure I wouldn't be forgiven if I tossed out things without due consideration."

Nicole drew about her the warmth his gaze lit inside her. "Tell Gram about the box we found with your name on it."

His gaze held hers another heartbeat, and then he turned to Gram. "Nicole is referring to a box of cards and letters. They were all addressed to me but had been returned."

"Returned?" Gram said. "I don't understand."

"It seems Aunt Millie tried to keep in touch with Ace after all, but her efforts had been refused."

Ace carefully closed the photo album and pushed it aside. "I found a letter that helps explain it." He cleared his throat.

Nicole could almost reach out and touch the brittleness coming from him. How she ached to be able to comfort him with her arms and her kiss. Except she wouldn't allow that to happen until he came back to his faith.

"From what I can piece together, it sounds as if Aunt Millie tried to gain custody of me. The letter said the authorities decided her health and age made it impossible. And in respect for the foster parents' wishes on my behalf"—his voice spiked with sarcasm and perhaps bitterness—"they asked that she not contact me anymore."

Shocked silence echoed through the room.

"Oh, Ace." Nicole didn't try to keep the sorrow from her voice.

"That's just so wrong," Carrie muttered.

Nicole took a look at Gram and, at the sight of tears trickling down her cheeks, sprang to her side. "Gram, don't cry."

Gram waved Nicole back to her seat. "Ace, I wish we could turn back the clock and save both you and Millie from such needless pain." She shook her head. "If only Millie had told us about it. Maybe we could have helped."

Ace folded his hand over Gram's. "Thank you for your concern, but don't be crying over me. Look at me. I turned out just fine, didn't I?"

Gram studied Ace carefully. "I suppose you did."

He smiled and began to turn away when Gram added, in a gentle voice, "At least on the outside. But it's the inside that counts, and I sense you felt abandoned, rejected, and hurt. How you've dealt with it I can't say, though it seems you've chosen a career where you don't have a chance to get close to people. Is that your way of protecting yourself from being hurt again?"

A visible shock raced through Ace's body. For a moment Nicole thought he would soften. Perhaps confess how much he longed for the things he'd been denied—family and security. But then he pushed himself against the back of the chair. His eyes revealed nothing.

❧

Ace banked his feelings. With Gram's injury and the pleasant afternoon then sharing a family meal, he'd let himself relax too much.

Okay, it had been a real shock to read that letter and have indisputable evidence Aunt Millie cared. But for whatever reasons, despite his desperate prayers to God for help, a home had been denied him. It no longer mattered. He'd given up his dreams. He'd stopped believing in miracles and a God who sent them.

He'd grown up. He'd learned to put aside his resentment and bitterness, but he could almost taste the poor-Ace feeling of the three females facing him. All pity and concern. But then they believed in forever families and happily ever after. He didn't. He believed in accepting the truth. Dealing with realities.

"I have a very good job because I worked hard and climbed to the top. I'm good at what I do." He had no intention of telling them the exact nature of some of the things he did, certain all three of them would consider a few of the situations he'd found himself in to be much too risky. They certainly had their reasons to worry about the safety of those they cared about, but he didn't fall into that category. They, at least, still had each other. What would it be like to have someone to care whether or not he took risks? He couldn't imagine.

Pretending to move the old photo album away from a speck of dirt on the table, he thought about Nicole. Would she ever consider accepting someone like him—a risk taker, a man with no experience of family? Not likely.

"I didn't mean to criticize what you do," Gram said. "I'm sure you're very good at your job. But then I expect you'd be good at whatever you set your mind to."

"Thank you." He had no intention of taking this conversation any further.

He turned to Nicole, narrowing his eyes with the cold distant look he'd perfected over a lifetime.

She met his look squarely, determination blaring from hers.

He got lost in the darkness of her gaze, swirling into unfamiliar territory filled with desires that were uniquely emotional rather than physical. He jerked a breath across his teeth and forced it into his gasping lungs. Time for reality.

"You coming to see what I found today?" His mind filled with thin cotton balls. He couldn't think. What treasures had he uncovered? The only thing he could remember was how her lips tasted like honey.

"Whose turn is it to do dishes?" Carrie demanded.

Nicole blinked and turned toward her younger sister.

Ace gave himself a mental shake. He could not let old photos, old memories, and old dreams put him off balance.

"I did them about four days in a row, so I'd say it was your turn," Nicole said.

"I guess." Carrie sighed.

"I'd offer to help, but I think I'll take advantage of my injury and watch the news." Gram pushed to her feet.

Ace helped her to the living room. When he returned, Nicole nodded toward the door, silently suggesting they leave, but seeing the disappointment in Carrie's expression he filled the sink with hot water and plunged in a stack of dishes.

"Many hands make short work," he said.

Nicole rolled her eyes but grabbed a cloth and dried the dishes as Carrie speedily finished clearing the table.

"This is great, Ace," Carrie said. "Thanks for helping."

Appreciation glistened in Nicole's eyes, and Ace smiled to himself. Seems doing a kindness for her sister or grandmother was a shortcut to earning Nicole's approval, although it hadn't been his motivation, nor would he ever allow it to be. He knew there was a reverse lesson to be heeded, as well. Neither would she forgive anyone who hurt them in any way. The whole family was fiercely protective of one another.

"Is that everything?" He glanced around before he pulled the plug and stood with his hands dripping over the sink.

Nicole offered him a corner of her tea towel.

"Thank you," she whispered. "That was very kind."

He held her gaze. "I'm your ordinary, everyday, kind sort of guy."

Her eyes darkened. "Not so ordinary, I think." Her voice purred.

"Want to come see the stuff I've discovered?" He was talking about the antiques that kept springing from the corners of the house, but his thoughts were not on looking at antiques. He had his mind on discovering a different sort of treasure. Nicole. He wanted to know everything about her.

❧

Nicole hurried outside to the shelter of the summer dusk. She didn't know if she could trust the way she felt. She needed to examine her reactions and base her choices on what was best. Reality. Security. Not on how her heart did a happy dance against her rib cage.

She should never have allowed herself to dream of what would happen when—

All through dinner, every time she looked at him, her heart did a funny little jump that set her pulses racing. Fearing Carrie or Gram would read the longing in her expression, she allowed herself only glances. A short intense meeting of the eyes. Or a skimming glimpse of his face to study the appealing stern lines around his eyes. Several times she reminded herself not to stare.

She needed distance. But she couldn't say whom she needed it from—Ace or herself.

Ace followed her outside, grabbed her hand, and pulled her to a stop. "What's your hurry? Let's enjoy the weather."

They reached the shadows of the alley, and she allowed

him to pull her into his arms. She'd been longing for this the whole evening. And all day. In fact, probably most of her life. She realized she'd subconsciously measured all her boyfriends against Ace and the way their hearts and minds seemed to knit together perfectly.

He murmured her name, turning her insides into cappuccino delight. Laughing, she ducked away from his kiss, allowing herself to stroke his cheek gently.

The lowering sun reflected in his eyes. Tenderness filled her. Of his own admission he'd never known love—the sort of love that endured. But one thing she was good at was loving. She would do her best to love him back to God and family. She took his hand and headed toward Aunt Millie's house. Reason must prevail. She had priorities. First, her faith. She would never love a man who didn't trust and serve God. And, second, her family. She would never jeopardize their security and happiness.

She stepped inside and hurried toward the dining room but barely noticed the additions, absently picking things up and turning them over without really seeing them.

Ace followed, stopping a thin inch behind her. She felt his warmth on her back. She closed her eyes and breathed in his scent. As he murmured her name, her heart opened up to him.

This was what God had intended when he created man and woman. This was how love was meant to be—connection to a man on one side and to family on the other.

Only God and family were not yet in Ace's vocabulary, and until they were, this love could not be.

Slowly she slipped from his grasp. "Let's see what you've uncovered today." She hurried to the collection on the table. "I need to start cataloguing and pricing things."

six

The next day Nicole answered the phone as it rang in her store.

"Hi. It's me. Ace."

She recognized his voice immediately and smiled. "Hi." She turned her back to the shop, hoping no one noticed her far-from-businesslike tone.

"The reason I called is I found a whole stack of boxes in the basement, full of old dishes and stuff. I've no idea if they're worth anything or if I should pitch the whole lot in the Dumpster."

"Don't dump anything until I see it." She glanced around the store. The shop was quiet. Rachel, her capable assistant, dusted a display. She checked her watch. An hour and a half until closing time.

"I could come over right away and have a look." She'd rather spend the time exploring old boxes with him than trying to get rust stains out of tiny crevices of the cut-glass candy dish she'd been cleaning in the back room.

She'd spent most of the day telling herself repeatedly her attraction to him could mean nothing until she got her miracle. But she couldn't deny how much she enjoyed just being with him. They shared a connection as old and familiar as her childhood. She felt comfortable and complete. . .odd word choice, but it had been the same when they were kids.

"I'm going to check out some antiques," she told Rachel.

"Close up for me, will you?"

Rachel turned and stared. "O—kay." She dragged out the word.

Nicole hurried away before Rachel could speculate about her leaving early. But, after all, it was work related. She was on a buying expedition.

She hurried along the streets keeping to the shady side, out of the hot sun. Heat waves shimmered off the pavement.

She knocked at Aunt Millie's back door and heard Ace's voice from deep inside the house.

"Come in."

She found him in the small room where Aunt Millie once slept. The bed had been dismantled several days ago and, along with several boxes of bedding, picked up by a charity. A dozen or more boxes stood in the middle of the room. Dust tickled her nose.

He stood, his hands on his hips staring down at a box with the flaps opened.

She chuckled softly, and he looked up, surprised. "What?"

"You have dust on your nose."

He stuck his hand into the short sleeve of his grungy T-shirt and wiped his face. Done, he grinned at her. "Better?"

"Much." She'd given herself a good talking to on the way over. This thing between them had to be put on hold. But she couldn't help the way her heart caught halfway up her throat at the way he looked at her, his expression gentle, his eyes smiling.

She tore her gaze away and looked at the boxes. "What do we have here?"

"I don't know for sure. I've only opened a few. Old dishes,

like I said. And bits and pieces of cloth and buttons. Looks like junk to me."

She knelt at the box with open flaps, flipped one side back and read OLD DISHES. "There you go. Just like you said. Let's have a look." The dishes had been neatly packed with layers of newspaper between that crumpled as she touched it. She gasped as she pulled a plate out. "It's a Willow." She turned it over. "A Dimmock."

He squatted beside her. "I take it that's good?"

"I'd have to check it out, but this plate is probably worth over two hundred dollars."

She put it aside and uncovered the next layer. Six small square plates followed by a rectangular tray with pierced side handles. Again she checked the back stamp. "These are authentic Burgess and Leigh. It's a sandwich set."

She dug further and uncovered more old Willow dishes. "Someone had quite a collection." She sat back on her heels, stunned at the discovery. "It's worth a lot of money."

She packed them back as carefully as she'd removed them and put the box out of the way. Then she turned and rubbed her hands with glee. "What else do we have?"

In the next box she uncovered a complete child's tea set in German china. "This is in perfect condition."

Ace opened the next box. "Old magazines." He sounded disappointed and began to shove the lot aside.

"Wait a minute." She checked the publication dates and condition. "These will sell well, too."

"This is the one full of buttons and junk."

Nicole wasn't about to disregard anything at this point. "Not just buttons and junk," she said, after looking through the contents. "Antique fabric and collectible buttons." They continued to open boxes. Each one had been carefully packed, cryptically labeled, and was full of treasures.

"This doesn't seem like Aunt Millie's stuff," she said. "I didn't see any of her boxes packed so carefully."

"It says Uncle Fred and Aunt Ina on a couple of boxes. I think she must have inherited this stuff. It doesn't look as if she ever unpacked it, though."

Nicole laughed. "She probably wondered where she'd put it." She sat comfortably on the floor surrounded by the now closed boxes, the smell of dust and old newspapers filling her nose. "This is quite a find. I'll do some research and see what it's worth. But I think both you and I stand to make a nice little profit from selling it."

He sat cross-legged a few inches from her and grinned. "Who'd have guessed such a dark, unfriendly place as the basement hid such treasures?"

"It's a miracle nothing's been damaged by dampness." She was grateful for the fact, but there was a miracle that would mean more to her than undamaged antiques or the profit they would generate. She leaned forward over her knees. "Ace, this house is full of treasures. And I don't mean the antiques. I'm thinking of Aunt Millie's letters to you and the letter to her explaining why she couldn't come and bring you home. But I'm also thinking of what else you had here." She offered a quick prayer that God would give her the words to say and Ace the heart to hear her. "I remember your faith in God. I remember how determined you were to be a Christian soldier." She locked eyes with him. His gaze cooled, grew distant, but she pressed on. "I know you figured your aunt abandoned you. And you were mistaken. Isn't it the same with God?"

She watched and waited, but his expression revealed only

detachment. Then he smiled. A condescending little grimace.

"I waited for a miracle." His voice was soft but flat, emotionless. "I prayed that God would make sure Aunt Millie came and got me. It never happened." He shrugged. "I stopped hoping. I stopped praying." He paused. "I stopped believing."

"Believing what? In God? Family? Prayer? People? What?"

"All of the above, I suppose. I count on no one but myself."

She jerked back, hurt by his words. "You don't trust me?"

She sat perfectly still as he studied her, smiled self-consciously as his gaze came to rest on her face and prayed he would see his judgment was wrong.

"I guess if I trust anyone it would be you."

Her breath eased out of tight lungs. "Why would you choose to trust me?"

"Because you haven't changed." His smile lit his face, ignited an answering glow inside her. "You're just as enthusiastic, caring, intense, and idealistic as when you were a kid."

She nodded. "Because that's who I am." What a perfect opening to turn this subject toward God. *Oh, Lord, help me use this. Give me the right words. Open his heart.* "And not changing is important to you?"

He considered it a moment. "Perhaps it's knowing I won't turn around and be surprised by something."

She wasn't sure she liked sounding about as interesting as an old standby chair, but right now that didn't matter. She wanted to explore how and what had shaped him into the man who sat before her, his expression half amused, half guarded. "Do you mean surprised in a bad way?"

"Yeah. Like finding out something that would make me wonder if I'd been mistaken in all the things I thought I understood about you." His voice deepened. "But as I said, you've grown up in a real good way. You're the same, only matured. I like what I see, what I'm discovering."

His words pleased her. Made her feel special. Not an old chair at all but something precious. Like one of these fine pieces of china. "Thank you. When Aunt Millie didn't rescue you, I guess you were disappointed and blamed God. But, Ace, God hasn't changed. He is the same yesterday, today, and forever. His promises never fail. He does not change His mind."

Ace's mouth set into a hard, unyielding line. "Then I know where I stand with Him."

She gasped. "You think He doesn't love you because of the bad things that happened." She shook her head hard. "You are so wrong."

"Yeah?"

"Yes. It isn't God who made the bad choices, but some humans with little compassion. And just as Aunt Millie didn't stop loving you, neither did God." She took a deep breath and plunged on even though she wondered if she might offend him. "Ace, you could have come back to Aunt Millie anytime after you were on your own. But you decided not to. You robbed yourself of the chance to know her love."

He sat as motionless as something made out of bronze. Not a flicker of motion in his face or sign of emotion in his eyes.

Praying again for wisdom, she rushed on. "You're doing the same with God. You're running from His love when you could return to it anytime you choose."

She stared into his gaze and waited. For several heartbeats she thought he was going to act as if he hadn't heard, and then he blinked. "You make it sound so easy."

"It is."

"Only for someone like you. Things have changed. I've changed. Aunt Millie is gone. It's too late."

"Ace, it's never too late."

But he pushed to his feet. "Want to look at the other stuff I unearthed today?"

She scrambled to her feet and glanced at her watch. "Look at the time. Gram will be wondering what happened to me." She headed for the door. "Maybe I can come back later?" Did she sound too eager?

"Sure. I'll be here."

"Better yet, join us for supper. Unless you have something planned." She glanced around the kitchen but saw only a can of coffee, a half-used loaf of bread, and an open jar of peanut butter. She nodded toward the fridge.

He grinned immediately. "It's empty except for butter and cheese. I haven't bothered much with food."

"Then come over. Gram will have supervised Carrie in preparing something."

"How's your grandmother today? Did you persuade her to see a doctor?"

Nicole laughed. "She said her ankle wasn't hurting very much so we compromised. She promised to stay off it if I didn't make her go to the doctor."

Ace chuckled. "Stubborn, is she?"

"She prefers to call it strong natured. You'll come?"

He nodded. "Give me time to shower."

❧

Ace tugged a clean shirt over his head, paused to check his hair, and decided he looked presentable enough to join the ladies for dinner. He might have refused if he wasn't so hungry and fed up with cheese.

He snorted. Sure he would have. He wanted to see Nicole every chance he got even though his instincts warned him he was playing with fire.

Normally he listened to his instincts. But not this time. This time his interest in one special little lady drowned out the voice of reason. She intrigued him with her fervent beliefs and loyalties.

Next door, Carrie and Gram greeted him warmly. Nicole stood back and smiled, happy to see him, or was she happy because her family brightened in his presence?

Whatever. He enjoyed the company of all three women. And if it made Nicole happy, it was good enough for him.

"I made porcupine meatballs for supper," Carrie announced. "With mashed potatoes and peas. It's my specialty."

Gram chuckled. "She makes it every time she has to make supper. Good thing we like it."

Ace turned to Gram. "How's your ankle?"

Gram darted a look at Nicole. "It's fine. I'm only keeping it up because I promised my granddaughter."

Nicole rolled her eyes.

Ace grinned, feeling amusement in the pit of his stomach.

"It's ready," Carrie announced. Gram allowed Ace to help her to the table, favoring her sore ankle more than she would ever admit.

After grace, they dug in.

Ace tried the meatballs. "Very good."

Carrie beamed, and Nicole sent Ace a grateful glance.

After the meal Carrie hurried out to a babysitting job. She paused at the door. "I got a new CD if you want to check it out."

Gram hobbled to the small sitting room off the kitchen to watch the news.

Nicole laughed. "Guess I'm stuck with dishes."

"I'll help."

"You don't have to. You're a guest."

Guest? The word echoed inside his chest making him aware of the dark, empty corners. If he allowed himself to be honest, he would be forced to admit he wanted to be more than a temporary guest. He shoved the idea away and started to stack dishes. "I want to help."

As they worked side by side, she told him of her plans to add more display shelves to her store and do a feature on the antiques. He enjoyed her enthusiasm.

They finished the dishes. He hung the towel neatly and leaned against the edge of the counter.

She stood in front of the sink, her back to the window, and watched him uncertainly.

He should go. But more dusty boxes held no appeal.

"You want to hear Carrie's CD?" she asked.

"Sure." That beat unpacking boxes any day. Especially with Nicole to keep him company. They went through the TV room where Gram sat with her head back, her eyes closed. Nicole held a finger to her lips as they tiptoed into the larger living room.

A huge old-fashioned stereo sat against one wall. An entertainment center next to it held a modern stereo with a collection of CDs in a stack. Ace bent, read the labels, not recognizing most of the names, then turned to the older machine and ran his fingers along the wooden cabinet. "This is beautiful."

"Gram's. I think she's had it since she got off the ark."

"Does it have a needle?"

Nicole struggled to get the plastic wrap off the CD. "Yup.

She still plays the records."

"May I look?"

Nicole shrugged.

He lifted the lid. The phonograph looked to be in excellent condition. One side of the cabinet was full of records. He checked the labels. "Wow. What a collection. George Beverly Shea to Elvis." He read the Elvis titles. "I used to know all the Elvis songs." At one time he did a pretty fair Elvis imitation, and to prove it he sang a few bars from each song on the record he held.

She sat back and grinned at him.

"Sing with me," he said.

She shook her head. "I don't know the songs."

He lowered the record cover and stared at her. "You don't know them?" He did his Elvis voice. "Well, baby, there's no time like the present."

She giggled. "I thought we were going to listen to Carrie's CD."

He shrugged and returned the record to the cabinet and sadly said, "Elvis has left the building." He lingered at the stereo, loathe to put Elvis to rest, then sat on the couch.

Still laughing, Nicole pushed the CD into the modern machine then sank to the floor close to his knees. A drum solo began and then a female voice. Nicole sang along, her voice strong and clear, as beautiful and sweet as Nicole herself.

The song was unfamiliar, but the words were distinct. All about God and worship and peace and love. He tried to block the words from his mind so he could enjoy listening to Nicole.

The song ended.

"What do you think?" Nicole asked.

"It's not Elvis."

"No, but she has something Elvis couldn't seem to find—peace."

"You got me there."

Nicole tipped her head. "It's too bad. Seems like he knew about God, just didn't *know* Him. Not in a way that made a difference to how he felt."

"Guess it just didn't work for him. Not everyone can believe like you do—in family, God, miracles, and happily ever after. I can't."

She shifted to stare at him. "I don't understand. You have proof you were wrong about Aunt Millie. Isn't that enough?"

"It isn't just Aunt Millie. Or even the foster care system. Have you ever seen a child with his belly swollen to the point of pain, his eyes glazed as he slowly starves to death? Have you seen other children crying and alone because their parents have been killed by guerrillas? Or worse, by AIDS?"

"And that's God's fault?"

"He could stop it."

"I suppose He could. But how long before man found something more cruel, more devastating, to do? There's nothing worse than man's inhumanity toward man."

He didn't reply. If God was all-powerful, He could stop it.

Nicole pulled herself up to the couch and sat beside him, turning so she could face him as she talked. She practically vibrated with intensity. Her face glowed with enthusiasm; her eyes sparkled. "Ace, have you looked as hard for evidence of God's love?"

Only his years of practice at giving away nothing at negotiations enabled him to meet her look without flinching. Her question caught him off guard. He, the mediator of many tense situations, the one who tried to find a reasonable middle ground, who prided himself on being able to see both sides, had not once looked for a balanced view of God.

His whole life was built on believing he needed no one, wanted nothing. Bit by bit, brick by brick, Nicole was tearing down his resistance. Aunt Millie, Nicole and her family, perhaps even God if he let himself believe the things Nicole said—each doing their part to peel back the layers he'd built around his heart, exposing it to things he'd closed himself to for years. But where did that leave him? Who was he if he tore away everything he'd built his life on?

"Come to church with me," she whispered.

He nodded, unable to resist her gentle invitation. He inched forward, wanting to kiss her sweet mouth.

She edged away, just out of reach.

"Nicole," Gram called from the other room. "Are you there?"

"Yes, Gram."

"Can you help me to bed?"

Nicole sprang to her feet. "I'll be right there." She stopped and smiled at Ace. "Her ankle is bothering her even if she won't admit it."

He rose slowly. They stood a few inches apart. He searched her gaze, found a welcome there. And more. A belonging? A connection begun eighteen years ago? He wasn't sure. But whatever it was felt good and right.

"I'll be on my way," he said. "Are you coming over later?"

She hesitated, glanced at her watch. "Maybe not. It's already late."

Disappointed, he touched her cheek, wishing for more. But Gram called again.

"I'll see you tomorrow then?" His husky voice revealed how much he regretted having to end this evening so soon.

She nodded.

❧

Ace leaned closer to the mirror and adjusted his tie. The past few days had been wonderful. All he'd ever imagined life could be. For the first time since his visit to Aunt Millie one long ago Christmas season, he enjoyed a sense of belonging. The Thomas family, as fun as it was loving, opened up and drew him into their circle. Pulled him in and made him part of themselves without leaving any wrinkles or bulges to indicate his presence caused any disturbance.

He rearranged the knot of his tie, even though it already lay perfectly centered, then turned from side to side to check his reflection.

The short-sleeved white shirt would have to do. He hadn't come prepared with anything dressier. He flicked a strand of hair off his forehead and hurried across the yard to the Thomas house.

Nicole opened the door at his knock. "You're early." Pink stole across her cheeks. Pleased to see he'd caught her thinking of him, he brushed at the blush with his knuckles.

"Just couldn't wait another minute," he teased, though the words held nothing but truth. The daytime hours passed on snails' tails while she worked at the store and he pretended to sort out Aunt Millie's house. The task no longer demanded he hurry, because once he finished he would have to deal with his emotions, and right now he preferred to ride the current. So he whittled away the leaden hours until Nicole got home from work.

After supper, which he shared with the family, he and

Nicole hurried to his house where the hours raced past like an Indy 500 event. They tried to concentrate on sorting and cataloguing Aunt Millie's valuables, but it took only minutes for them to be lost in conversation. He wanted more, but she always ducked away when he tried to kiss her.

He studied her now.

"Carrie, are you ready?" Gram called from the living room; then she and Carrie joined them.

Tightness gripped Ace's collarbone. Suddenly he was tense. Welcoming him in the privacy of her home was one thing. Going out in public quite another. He, of all people, knew that. How many times had foster families left him out of their activities? And yet she took his arm as they turned toward the door.

She felt exactly right at his side. As if she'd been born for that place next to his heart. He wanted to jump to the moon. Swing through the trees beating his chest. Warning lights flashed at the back of his mind reminding him of his vow to avoid the emotional quicksand this feeling signaled. He resolutely ignored the warning. For just now, while he cleaned out the house, he would allow himself to experience belonging and acceptance.

"Is everyone ready?" Gram beamed as she looked around. "Carrie, we'll walk together." Her ankle already better, she marched the girl out the door leaving Ace and Nicole to follow.

Nicole laughed softly. "Thank you, Gram."

Gram didn't turn around but nodded her head briskly.

For Ace, it was a walk to remember: the summer sun warm on his skin, the sky like a big blue tent, the birds an exuberant orchestra. A feeling in his heart as big as the whole outdoors. *So this is what it feels like to belong?*

He let the idea seep through his brain, ignoring the insistent warning accompanying it. *Better be prepared for disappointment.* He pressed Nicole's hand closer so he felt its reassuring warmth against his ribs and dismissed the uneasy little tremor in his brain.

Nicole waved at a family across the street but kept her other hand on his arm for all to see.

Life had finally turned around. All the things he'd ached for when he was a boy and put aside as a man now seemed within easy reach.

Trouble was, he didn't trust easily.

He didn't need a clout to the side of the head to know what bothered him. He and Nicole were as unlikely a match as anyone could imagine. She with her idealistic views of life and family, he with his jaded approach. Their lives had taken them in opposite directions. She was permanency, promises, safety—all things he wasn't. She believed finding a box of cards and letters proving Aunt Millie tried to keep in touch with him erased the years of feeling he didn't belong.

Sure, it felt good to know the old gal had tried. And suddenly a lot of things fell into place—the restrictions on the use of the telephone, the glances between the adults when he asked about mail. But it was only a part of what had gone into shaping him.

They reached the church steps. Nicole introduced him to those they met. Hands extended and welcomed Ace before they took their places in the polished wooden pews.

The muted light from the pebbled glass windows bathed Nicole in a warm glow. The room radiated with love. Or was it confined to Ace and the girl at his side? If love felt like this he ought to bottle the feeling and sell it.

Nicole's voice rang out clear and sweet as they sang hymns.

The pastor stood to the pulpit. "My text for today is John 15, verse 13, 'Greater love hath no man than this, that a man lay down his life for his friends.' God did more than that. He loved us and sacrificed His dear Son while we were enemies. His love knows no boundaries, no excuses, no limits. And yet how many of us run from this great love rather than opening our hearts to it? My question is, how far can you run from God and His love? Psalm 139 says, 'If I ascend up into heaven, thou art there. . .if I take the wings of the morning. . .'"

Ace sat back as if something heavy and hard had slammed into his chest. Was he running from God's love? The very thing he yearned for but feared to trust? Had God pursued him all these years waiting to pour love into his life? Had He brought him back to Reliance for that reason? To discover Aunt Millie had cared, Nicole and her family still cared? To find a place where he belonged? Was this what God had in mind for him? Something warm and fluid washed over his insides. Was this feeling of well-being for real?

He didn't hear a lot of the sermon; yet, as he left the church, he knew he'd never had such a deeply religious experience. His heart beat stronger than he could remember it beating before. As if it had been lovingly caressed.

The four of them retraced their steps toward home.

"You'll have dinner with us, won't you, Ace?" Gram said. "I have a casserole in the oven."

"Gram's famous Sunday dinner casserole," Carrie said. "Chicken and rice and peas. Umm, umm, good."

"Unless you've got something more appealing at home." Nicole gave him a wide-eyed innocent look that didn't fool him for a minute. She knew the meager extent of his supplies.

Nicole knew how Gram's Sunday casserole tasted, but today it held none of the familiar comforting flavors. It could have been sawdust for all the enjoyment it gave her. Her whole being quivered with tension. Tears choked the back of her nose.

She'd been aware of Ace's startled reaction to the sermon. She knew it had touched his heart. Having Ace go to church with them and join them for dinner afterward felt so right. As if her whole life had shaped itself for this moment. She knew he was very close to believing in God's love.

"I'll do dishes," Carrie said, as they finished the apple crisp dessert.

Nicole's mouth dropped open at Carrie's uncharacteristic offer.

"Why don't you show Ace Mom and Dad's park?" Carrie added.

Nicole patted her sister's head. "Thank you, Carrie. That's so sweet."

She waited until Ace helped her step into his black SUV before she explained. "It's a public park, but Carrie likes to think it belongs to our family."

Following her directions, he turned left at the corner. The park lay on the outskirts of town. It had been a favorite place for campouts, wiener roasts, and picnics when her parents had been alive—her mother and second father. Since their deaths, she and Carrie and Gram made a yearly pilgrimage to remember the family they had once been.

"I have something special to show you." She pulled Ace toward the grove of trees close to the gurgling river. "See this?" She drew him to a tree and touched the carved initials.

Inside a heart were the initials of her mother and stepfather. In two smaller hearts were her initials and Carrie's. "Our family tree." She laughed awkwardly.

Ace trailed his fingers along the letters and shapes, a thoughtful look on his face. His words were low. "A literal family tree. Neat."

"It was Dad's idea." She turned to study the circle of trees, the rusted fire pot, the burnt logs, and the green picnic table marked with years' worth of initials and shapes carved into its top. "We used to come here so often. It's where he proposed to my mother. We came here when they got back from their honeymoon and had a special family ceremony. That's when he carved my initials in my heart." She closed her eyes and waited for her throat to relax so she could talk. "We came when Carrie was six weeks old. Dad held my hand and helped me put the initials in her heart." She stopped again and steadied her breathing. "There were supposed to be more hearts, but it never happened."

Ace wrapped his arms around her and pulled her to the bench of the picnic table. He pressed her face into the hollow of his neck and held her tight, crooning her name as she let the tears flow. They lasted only a minute. She didn't often cry for her parents anymore, although she missed them at unexpected times and places—Carrie's ball games, the opening of her store, when Aunt Millie died.

She quieted and rested contentedly in his arms, comforted by his sympathy.

"I'm not sure which is worse," he murmured. "To never have known family life or to have known it and lost it."

"Even knowing how things would turn out, I wouldn't give up a minute of our time together."

He didn't answer, but she felt his doubt.

She pushed back so she could see into his face. "I had a whole family for a lot of years. I had a father who loved me." Her voice dropped to a whisper. "I needed that. It made up for what I lost when my own father died." Her smile felt wobbly. "And now I have Carrie and Gram. What more could a person ask for?"

He looked deep into her eyes, searching, she was certain, for answers to his own doubts, answers to questions he perhaps couldn't even voice.

"Nicole, what happened to your father?"

She knew he didn't mean Paul Thomas but Nicolas Costello. She sat up straight, twisting her hands into a tight knot. "I was five years old. He promised to bring me a special present for my birthday. I waited and waited, but he never came." Nicole steadied her voice. This was old news. She'd dealt with it and put it behind her. It no longer had the power to turn her inside out. "He died in a reckless skydiving accident." Her voice hardened. Pain iced her veins. "He didn't have to. He was a risk taker and a gambler. His gambling left the restaurant heavily in debt. Mom had to sell it and move back here to Reliance to live with Gram." Her eyes burned with memories of her hurt, her anger that her father gambled away his life on some thrill rather than be there for her. She faced Ace. "His decisions were selfish. He didn't think about us. How we would feel when things went wrong."

Ace nodded slowly, his expression guarded. "That's why you're afraid of taking risks."

"I will never do anything to jeopardize my family's stability."

He trailed his finger over her cheek. "Maybe we are more alike than we know."

"How can that be? We're as different as black and white. My family is the most important thing in my life. You don't even want to believe in family. I always take the safe route. Your job requires you to take risks. I believe fervently in God's love. You doubt it. How much more different can we be?" And yet between them lay a bond of velvety steel she couldn't overlook. Something in her reached out and found belonging with him.

It was the way he slid into her family. And how his practical common sense soothed away her worries. He seemed to match her emotionally. And there was no denying an attraction between them.

"Perhaps opposites attract," he said. "Perhaps our differences complete each other. Perhaps we share more than we know."

She waited for him to explain.

"You see, my mother, too, made choices that cost her her life and me my security."

She digested his statement. "How did she die?"

"She chose to die by the bottle."

"What do you mean?"

"She drank herself to death. Literally."

"Oh, Ace, I'm so sorry. I just assumed she had cancer or something."

Silently they held hands. Her heart actually hurt with every breath. They'd both lost so much. And paid such a price for choices made by other people.

"You've lost more than me," she said. "At least I've always had my family. You had no one except Aunt Millie, and she couldn't reach you. How awful."

"Perhaps good has come of it."

She clenched his hand tighter. "How?" She prayed he'd see God's hand in his life.

"It forced me to deal with my bad attitude. I learned to look ahead instead of back. Living in a series of foster homes taught me how to deal with all sorts of people. It's made me who I am." He pulled her against his chest. "And life has taught you to be loyal, kind, and—"

"Cautious," she finished for him.

"So where does that leave us?"

"I'm not sure." She sighed. "I don't want to think about it. Can't we simply enjoy this moment?"

He chuckled. "Sounds more like something I would say."

She nodded. But right now she wanted to rest in the comfort of what they shared. She knew he'd been touched by the sermon this morning. She knew God was at work. She would see her miracle. Of that she had no doubt.

Later they wandered among the trees, enjoying the birds and flowers and small children playing. She longed to ask him about his experience in church but knew she had to be quiet and let God work.

seven

"Did you see this?" Rachel waved the newspaper in front of Nicole.

"Haven't looked at the news." She sat at her desk in the store, doodling on a slip of paper.

"Come on, girl. Get a grip. You've done nothing but moon around here for days. In fact"—Rachel leaned over to peer into Nicole's eyes—"I'd be inclined to say you were off in some dream world." She plucked the scrap of paper off the desk. "Ace. Oh ho. So that's it. Our elusive Nicole Thomas has fallen in love. And with a hard-eyed stranger at that."

Nicole snatched the paper back. "He's not a stranger. I've known him since I was ten." What possessed her to scribble his name in the margins?

Rachel perched on the desk. "Nope. It's love. Not that I blame you. He's quite the looker."

"I'm not in love." She wouldn't let herself think that. Even if he turned back to God, and she prayed he would, there was still his job to think about. She knew he encountered dangerous situations. Oil well fires, ecoterrorists, jungle fever, and who knew what else. Not the sort of risks she wanted to deal with or subject her family to.

"Nicole, sweetie, it's me you're talking to. Your best friend. Do you really think I haven't noticed the starry look in your eyes lately?" She chuckled. "I always knew you'd fall hard when you fell, but I never thought you'd go for a—well, what can I say? He's an adventurer. He'll drag you away from your safe little world. And about time, I'd say."

Rachel's words stung. She made it sound as if Nicole lived in a state of denial, locking herself in a padded cell or something. "I'm not about to leave my family, no matter what. I would never do that to them."

"Uh-huh." Rachel's look of resignation was the last straw.

"What's so interesting in the newspaper?" Conversation closed. End of subject.

Rachel sighed once then flipped the paper open to reveal an article. "That wonderful little woodcarver is selling out."

Nicole skimmed the article. Only a few lines in the back of the arts and entertainment section buried in a column about what's new and hot in the local galleries. But if anyone had seen his work, they'd be beating a path to his door. She tapped her finger on the paper. "I've always wanted to get more of his work." She glanced around the store. "If I could buy him out—" Jumping to her feet, she circled the room. "Just picture his wild animal carvings on some shelves against this wall. I could hang Aunt Millie's linens on a rack over here and move the paintings to the stair wall." She raced up the steps, mentally measuring the space. "I have to get there before anyone else," she called over the wooden banister she'd sandpapered and polished inch by inch until it looked as good as the day her grandfather had installed it.

Rachel bounced off the desk and leaned against the banister watching. "I doubt any city dude will find the place. It took us hours to find that little log cabin. We would have driven right past it if we hadn't known what we were looking for."

Nicole ground to a halt and descended the stairs. "That's right. But I want those things so bad. They're exquisite." The elderly man did extraordinary work, everything from chain-saw creations to tiny forest animals so delicate she held her breath so she wouldn't frighten them away. "What I wouldn't give to have some of those pieces right now." She didn't need a medical opinion to know Gram's cataract surgery needed to be done soon. She'd noticed how Gram counted the stitches on her knitting needle by feel rather than sight and how she opted to watch the news on TV rather than read the paper as had been her pleasure not so long ago. Nicole's income had increased with the addition of Aunt Millie's antiques, but her savings were growing too slowly for her liking. Getting the woodcarver's work would up her income substantially.

"Maybe you should go talk to him."

"You're right. I'm going to head out there this very minute." She studied the room again. "I want twice as much display space. Just think—I'll soon be making enough money for Gram's eye surgery and Carrie's university education." She grinned. "Maybe even new teeth for Gram."

"You go, girl. Grandpa's Attic is gonna be the best little art store in the West." She tilted her head and wrinkled her eyebrows. "Guess it isn't really an art store. Hmm. Not sure what to call it."

Nicole grinned. "I'll settle for your calling it 'best.'"

Just then the bell above the door jangled. Nicole turned to see who it was, and her knees weakened.

Ace stood framed in the door, his gaze searching the room until he found Nicole. Then a wide warm smile lit his face.

"Look at him," Rachel whispered out of the corner of her mouth. "He's got it as bad as you."

Nicole's pulse hammered in her throat as their gazes locked. It felt as if their hearts leapt across the room and collided.

Sudden heat rushed up her neck, and she couldn't speak.

"I think I'll make myself scarce," Rachel muttered. "But if I were you, I'd be asking the hunk to take you to see the woodcarver. Nothing like a nice drive in the country."

Nicole barely noticed Rachel march away as Ace crossed the room and stood before her.

"Hi." She couldn't look away from his eyes. The hazel irises seemed almost iridescent. "What are you doing here?" She grimaced. What a way to greet a prospective customer. But somehow she didn't think he'd come to buy something. "I mean, I thought we were to meet after work." They planned to watch Carrie's ball game this evening.

"I couldn't wait. Besides, I've never been inside your store, and I keep hearing all these great things about it. Thought I'd have a look around." But his gaze never shifted from hers.

She swallowed hard and glanced around the room. It looked like a place she'd never been before. How dumb was that? She knew this building from the tiny attic hole to the damp basement. With effort she jerked her brain back into gear. "Let me show you around." Her words rote, she described various objects. What was he really doing here? She led him up the stairs to the second level.

She lifted one of the pottery mugs she'd brought from the show in Great Falls. "Isn't this beautiful? Look at the lines. And the glaze. Shelley Brash is the artist. I fell in love with her work as soon as I saw it. I knew it would be a big hit, and it has been."

He studied the mug and nodded. "I can see why people would want it."

His appreciation loosened her thoughts.

"This building belonged to my grandfather," she explained.

"Since his death years ago, it went from being a hardware store to a grocery store and then a convenience store. I worked as a clerk here after I came back home. When the lease expired a year ago, Gram handed it to me and said to do what I wanted with it. And I did."

She told how she'd restored both the interior and exterior, discovered the plank floor under layers of carpet, linoleum, and paint, and polished it to a fine patina then created what she hoped were attractive displays.

His eyes widened with appreciation. "You've done a lot of work."

She sucked in warm air and grinned. "I don't mind the work. I love the beautiful things I've found. Some of them I hate to see go. But that's the whole deal. Buy beauty. Sell beauty. And hope to pay the bills." Right now she was barely breaking even, but that would change as she took in more and more stock. First, the lovely things from Aunt Millie's, and if she could get the woodcarvings. . .

If only she could scoop up the entire lot before anyone else discovered them. What a draw that would be.

She pointed out the antiques she'd cleaned and displayed. "These are going over big as well. I love telling people how I knew Aunt Millie and little things I remember about each item. I hope the stories and memories will go home as well. Maybe keep a bit of Aunt Millie alive."

"That's important to you, isn't it?" His eyes looked far away as if trying to distance himself from that part of his life.

"Yes, it is." She tugged his arm and pulled him back to her. "Maybe someday you'll admit family is important to you, too."

His eyes narrowed, and then a slow smile widened his mouth. "I'm learning to appreciate family. Yours. Not mine.

It's too late for me to have that."

She nodded, slowly, reluctantly. Aunt Millie was gone. They'd never had a chance. "I don't mind sharing my family with you."

He smiled. "So what's a smart businesswoman like you doing right now?"

She grabbed up the newspaper. "I was planning to head out to see this man." Remembering Rachel's words, she said, "Would you like to come along?"

"Woodcarver? Would I?"

She laughed. "No wood eyes, just wood animals."

He blinked, then laughed as he followed her outside. "Do you have directions?"

"Yup." She tapped her head, hoping she could find her way again.

"My vehicle's here. We'll take it." He'd driven his SUV to the store and hurried around to open the door for her. Following her directions, he turned his truck to the west and headed toward the mountains. She concentrated on the road, watching for some sign to indicate where to turn.

"North here," she said, hoping she was right. The road was barely a trail. Almost invisible. Just as she remembered it.

He slowed to make a corner.

She leaned forward to peer out the window. "Very few people have been able to find this place. Wait until you see the work the old man does. It's like nothing you've ever seen. If I can buy his entire business, not only will I stand to make a nice profit, I'll corner the market." She grinned at him. "It would be like a gift from heaven."

He shot her a puzzled look. "I never figured you to care so much about making money."

She concentrated on the road. "It's not for me. It's for Gram and Carrie." She told of their needs. "Carrie will make an excellent teacher."

"There it is." She pointed to a tiny weathered sign—LOST IN THE WOODS. The cabin was almost completely hidden among the trees.

"Appropriate name," he murmured. "This is really the back of beyond."

She nodded, eyes forward. "If it was any easier to get to, this man would have a world-wide reputation."

They pulled into a tiny clearing. A narrow log cabin faced them, weathered gray with age, flowers crowding up to the walls.

"Isn't it beautiful?" she whispered.

He agreed as they climbed the low verandah and pushed open the heavy door. A bell chimed overhead as they entered a narrow room. Along one wall stood large carvings of trees and bears and deer. Two of the other walls had sturdy shelves filled with smaller items. The nearest carving made Nicole hold her breath, and she touched Ace's arm to get his attention: A tiny deer poised under a spruce tree. She reached out, knowing it wasn't real yet needing to touch it to convince herself.

Nicole signaled Ace to wait, and they stood at the doorway not speaking until a tiny woman shuffled through the far door.

"I'm sorry." Her voice sounded like the wind sifting through the treetops. "We're no longer open for business."

"Mrs. Garnier, it's me, Nicole Thomas. I bought a set of birds from you earlier. Lovely work. I saw in the paper that you're selling out."

The old lady settled to a chair. "Hate to let it go but haven't got a choice. Arman's getting too old." She dabbed at her eyes. "He can barely see anymore. Forgets what he's doing. Almost cut his hand off t'other day."

"I'm sorry." Nicole spoke softly.

The older woman's cloudy eyes went around the room, lingering on item after item.

"Can't hardly bear to part with 'em but can't take 'em with us. Moving into a little place. What they call them places? Condos? No room. No room at all. But close to our daughter."

"I'm so sorry. Is the business still for sale?" Nicole hated to add to the woman's distress, but she didn't want some city fellow snatching the treasures from under her nose.

"One young man from the city came."

Nicole's breath jerked into her chest. Was she too late? She reached for Ace's hand, needing something to cling to.

The old woman shook her head. "He was so high and mighty. I hate to think of him taking our creatures. All he could talk about was how much money they'd make him. We didn't like that, did we, Arman?"

An old man shuffled through the door to his wife's side. He didn't respond to the question. Nicole was shocked to see how he'd deteriorated since her last visit.

"Are you still planning to sell them?" Nicole asked.

"Got to. Got to," the older woman muttered.

Nicole circled the room, picked up a bear here, a deer there, exclaimed over a squirrel holding a pinecone. She returned to the couple. Knowing she would never be able to afford the entire collection, she mentally picked out the pieces she'd like to have.

"I've always admired your work." She addressed the old man. "It's the most beautiful woodcarving I've ever seen. The animals almost seem to be alive, holding their breath, waiting for us to leave so they can get on with their work. I'd be honored to own some of your work."

The old woman took her husband's hand. "We want it to all go together. Wouldn't be right to separate them. We just want it over and done with. No hassling with a bunch of people."

"How much?"

The woman named a sum.

Nicole sighed. If only she hadn't depleted her savings at the Great Falls show. "It's a lot of money."

The old woman pushed to her feet and got a piece of paper from a desk in the corner. She handed the slip of paper to Nicole. Nicole studied it and nodded.

"Yes, I know. The price is more than fair. Would you consider letting me take it on consignment?"

The woman held her husband's hand. "You seem like the sort of person who would take proper care of our pets." She shook her head. "But we need the money. We have to pay for our condo."

Ace pulled his checkbook from his pocket. "I can see why you want this stuff. I'll lend you the money, and you can pay me the same as with Aunt Millie's stuff. As you sell it."

"No thanks." The look she gave him made him stuff the checkbook and pen back into his pocket.

The old man mumbled something. His wife looked long and hard at him then turned to Nicole. "We want you to have our pets. But we can't stay here much longer."

"I understand." She patted the old man on the shoulder.

"Arman wants me to give you two months to get the money."

Nicole nodded. "Thank you. I'll be back." She could barely

make it out of the cabin. Two months? How could she hope to earn that much money in such a short time? It was impossible. Back at the truck she faced Ace. "If I planned to borrow money, I would go to the bank."

Without waiting for his help, she jumped into the truck and shut the door.

He climbed in. "I was only offering to help."

She sighed. "I know. I didn't mean to snap at you, but I really want that collection." She sighed again. "I just don't have the money. And I doubt if I can raise it in two months. Truth is, it's more than I expect to earn from the store in six months. I was hoping. . ." She shrugged. She'd hoped they'd consider consignment or perhaps a down payment and then monthly installments. It was the only way she could afford to go. "Guess I set my sights too high. Still, it's the peak of tourist season, and with Aunt Millie's things I just might. . ." It would take a miracle. Seemed as if she wanted more than her fair share of them lately.

"Where does this road go?" He nodded in the opposite direction from which they'd come.

"I'm not sure. Maybe the river."

"Want to go find out?"

She nodded, still distracted by the business at the cabin.

In a few minutes the road ended. They got out and clambered over the rocks to the edge of the bank overlooking the river several feet below them. Ace chose a spot, and they sat on the ground, their backs against a fallen tree.

Nicole stared down at the river. "They're the most exquisite things I've ever seen. If only they didn't insist I pay for it all at once."

"Are they asking a fair price?"

"More than fair. Some of his work would bring a thousand dollars or more from the right buyer. Whoever gets it will stand to profit."

"So you're saying it's a sound business investment?"

She nodded.

"I'd be more than willing to lend you the money."

She made a protesting noise, but before she could speak he went on.

"But, as you're opposed to that, why not borrow the money from the bank? That's what they're for, you know."

"I don't borrow money. I promised myself I never would." But if she didn't, she would lose a wonderful business opportunity.

He studied her carefully. "Is this about your father?"

She shrugged and picked up a twig. "Going into debt cost my mother and me our security." She snapped the twig between her fingers. "His risk-taking cost him his life."

"You aren't your father, and there's a difference between foolish chances and an investment. To buy merchandise you know you can make a profit on is not a gamble. It's a business decision."

"I'd have to borrow against the store."

"You have nothing to lose, though. You buy the stuff. Sell it at a profit. Pay back the loan. In the meantime you have a unique and original collection drawing in customers so you sell even more—make more money. It isn't a gamble. It's a wise business choice."

She watched the water ripple past them.

"I don't know. I understand what you're saying but. . ." She sighed. "I just don't like to take risks."

"What risks?"

She grabbed another twig and twisted it round and round. "Borrowing money. What if. . . ?" She threw the twig into the water. "I would never do anything to hurt my family."

"And this would hurt them how?"

"I don't know." She flung herself down on her back and stared at the cloudless sky. "You're mixing me all up."

He leaned on one elbow, looking into her face. "It seems simple enough to me. Either you want the old man's carvings enough to get the money, or you decide it's easier to let them go."

"I want them."

"Then it's settled."

A mix of emotions played through her—uncertainty, fear.

She sighed. "You make it sound so simple."

"I'm not saying it's simple. Life is never simple. But sometimes it's necessary, and maybe even healthy, to step away from old habits. Even if the first step is scary."

"I need to think about it."

"Yes, you do. But you make me wonder if your faith in God is as real as you say it is."

She sat upright and stared at him. "Of course it is."

"Then maybe it's time to put it into practice."

She knew what he meant. "Take the risk and let God be in charge of whether it succeeds or fails?"

He settled back, as relaxed as could be while she felt ready to explode.

"Isn't that what trust is all about?"

"Not exactly. I think we're expected to make wise choices." This conversation filled her with confusion.

"Borrowing money is sometimes a wise choice. It certainly is here. If you don't get the money in a matter of weeks, someone else is going to buy that stuff, corner the market, and make a nice profit. I think"—he kept his voice soft and low—"you're afraid of risks. So afraid you can't even trust God."

She stared at him. "You're wrong." But even to her own ears she sounded uncertain. "I do trust God. In fact, I'm going to trust Him to help me raise the money in the next two months."

"By selling your merchandise?"

She nodded slowly. "I know it will take a miracle, but God is a God of miracles."

He plucked a feathery head of grass and brushed it across her arm. "So you prefer to make God do the work?"

She jerked away from the tickle of the grass. "Believe me, I'll be working."

"But if you don't get the money, it's God who failed to provide a miracle, rather than you who passed up a business opportunity God sent your way?"

"No. Hey, aren't I supposed to be trying to convince you to trust God, not the other way around?"

"Maybe you've done such a good job I've passed you."

He brushed the head of grass up her other arm. She snatched it from him and tossed it away.

"What did you say?" she demanded.

"I'm a quick learner?"

She leaned over, pinning his eyes with her gaze. "Tell me, Ace Conners—have you decided to trust God?"

His eyes reflected the dark pines around him. She sensed his uncertainty as he hesitated. "Almost," he whispered.

She cupped his cheek in her palm and laughed. "I truly believe in miracles. You are proof."

He quirked an eyebrow. "How so?"

"Since you came, I've been praying you would find your way back to faith."

"I said *almost*."

She let herself enjoy the feel of his warm skin, the roughness of his whiskers beneath her hand, then drew away. "At least you're headed in the right direction. And I'm going to trust Him for a miracle to buy Arman's collection, as well. That way I don't have to take any risks." She ignored the knowing look in Ace's eyes. Sure, to him it sounded like a cop-out, but no way would she borrow money and risk losing the store. Even if it looked like a certain thing. She knew better than to think anything was certain. She quickly amended her thought: except God's faithfulness.

Ace got up and pulled her to her feet. "We're going to be late for Carrie's game."

"No way. She'd never forgive us."

eight

Ace led her back to the SUV, and they made it to town just in time for the start of Carrie's game. He cheered and whistled each time Carrie caught the ball or batted.

Carrie waved and bowed and blew him kisses. Nicole grinned at the two of them.

But Ace's thoughts were busy elsewhere. Nicole couldn't have made it clearer that he didn't belong in her world. She didn't take risks. Period. Not even safe ones. And he was a risk. His job, his past, his views on life and living. Even his tentative trust in God. All constituted risks. Bad risks. If he had a lick of sense he would walk away this minute and never look back. Let a moving company come in and dispose of the rest of Aunt Millie's stuff.

But he didn't have the sense of a grasshopper.

Or maybe because he *was* a risk taker he didn't move on. He intended to hang around and see what happened—to his interest in Nicole, to her business, to his fledgling trust in God. Still too fragile to be called "trust," he wanted to see where things went. Not quite ready to commit himself to faith, he wanted proof. He wanted to see if God really cared about him, Ace Conners.

❧

"I've decided to call in a dump truck to clean out the garage," Ace said days later. "I don't feel like tackling another stack of boxes."

Nicole jerked back from washing dishes. "You can't do that. The place is full of wonderful antiques."

Ace shrugged. "I'm sick of poking through garbage for something that might be worth a few bucks." The whole business held no pleasure when he had to do it on his own. Set on raising money to buy Arman's collection, something he knew was impossible in the time frame allowed, Nicole spent every minute at the shop. She'd decided to stay open late and, rather than pay for help, stayed herself. The only way he got to see her at all was to invite himself over for the evening meal. And accompany them to church on Sunday. Not that either activity proved a hardship. The ladies were good company, and he eagerly listened to every word the preacher delivered. The consistent message seemed to be God's love and faithfulness. Ace found it easier and easier to believe it was true. Still, he wasn't one hundred percent convinced it applied to him.

Nicole sighed deeply. "Would it help if I lent a hand?"

He held back a smile. He figured she would go for the bait, but he wasn't about to let her know he'd set her up. "You don't have time."

"Rachel is always saying she'll put in a few more hours at the store. I could probably get her to stay until closing time a few nights."

He dried the last pot and stowed it in the cupboard before he answered. "I guess I could put off arranging a truck for another day."

A little frown hovering between her eyes, she grabbed the towel from him and wiped her hands. That tension hadn't existed before her visit to the woodcarver's cottage.

He touched her shoulders, bringing her gaze upward to his. "Nicole, when are you going to stop pushing yourself so hard?

You can't possibly raise enough money in two months. Go to the bank and borrow what you need. It's not a risk."

She clung to his gaze. He felt her determination. Her desperation. Heard it in her voice when she said, "It's only six weeks now."

"Which means you should have raised a quarter of the money. Have you?"

She looked panicked. "Not even an eighth. But something will happen. I just need to make some big sales."

"Nicole, you'd need to sell most of the stuff in your store."

Her eyes glistened with tears. "I need more stock."

"You need to stop trying to do this yourself. Let me help you. Or borrow the money from the bank."

She rocked her head back and forth. "I just can't take the risk."

The same old story. Nicole would never do anything she perceived to be risky. That included him. He would never really belong. Yet he couldn't walk away. He closed his eyes. Here in Reliance, in the warmth of her family and the belonging he felt with her and, yes, the way his heart opened toward God, he admitted he wanted to belong like he'd never wanted anything before.

Not true, he realized. He'd wanted it since he was a kid. He'd wanted a home. He'd wanted a family.

He'd been denied it by some nameless, faceless authority. And in his disappointment he'd shut God and love out of his life.

He headed for a repeat of the same disappointment if he kept hanging around waiting for Nicole to accept his devotion.

But he couldn't leave her struggling to live her safe little life. Perhaps losing the things she really cared about. Like Arman's work.

He pulled her into his arms, cradling her against his chest. He ached for her to belong there. He wanted to kiss away all her fears. But even though she pressed her face into his shirt and wrapped her arms around him like she was afraid to let go, she never allowed him to do anything more than give her a friendly kiss.

He kissed the top of her head and breathed in the smell of lemon and lilac from her hair.

She pushed away. "We better get at that garage."

Reluctantly he let her go.

❧

"Wanna come to Great Falls with me?" Ace asked Nicole as they examined the boxes in the garage. So far they'd found nothing she deemed of value. He could feel her discouragement and wanted to do something to ease it. Perhaps a trip away would help her regain her perspective.

"I have to go to the office for a few minutes," he said. "Then we could do something fun."

She sat back, a stunned look on her face. "You have an office in Great Falls? You've been less than an hour away all this time and we've never seen you?"

He chuckled. "Hardly. But I couldn't continue to ignore my work so I rented office space, and my secretary, Martha, has set up quarters so I can handle a few details."

She looked appeased then sighed. "I can't go. I have too much to do."

"When did work become the most important thing in your life?"

She made a protesting noise as she flipped open a box; then

her interest shifted away from Ace's question while she pulled out old bottles and examined them. "Finally something of value. These are in mint condition." She glanced up and met his gaze, looking thoughtful. "I know a gallery owner in Great Falls. I could see if he'd take some stuff on consignment. If I could double my sales. . ."

"So it's a yes?"

She shifted, scanned the remaining boxes, and sighed. "I'll have to get a bunch of stuff ready." She finger-brushed her hair. "But I don't know where I'll find the time."

"Could I help?"

She looked at him, right through him—he suspected to a mental view of her work—wondering perhaps if she dared accept his offer.

He nodded at the greenish jar in her hand. "I'm sure I can wash old bottles without breaking them."

Her gaze shifted back to focus on his eyes. A smile curved her lips. How he wanted to wipe that hint of anxiety from her expression. He wanted to hold her, take care of her, be here for her every day—

He jerked his thoughts back to reality. Just as he couldn't deny this sense of rightness between them nor how much he cared, neither could he build a future filled with nothing but dreams.

"I thought you were anxious to get this stuff cleaned out." She nodded to the unopened boxes and unexamined piles of stuff.

"A few more days won't make a world of difference. Let's go to your workroom right now, and I'll show you how handy I can be."

She put the green jar back in the box and closed the lid. "Let's take this."

He grabbed the box and headed for his SUV.

At the store Rachel, busy with an older couple studying one of the fabric art paintings, nodded hello to Nicole, her eyebrows shooting up when she saw Ace.

He followed Nicole into the back room and glanced around. "I see you've been busy."

"Every spare minute." She brushed past him to clear a space on her worktable.

He set the box on a nearby shelf and rubbed his hands together. "Show me what to do."

"I need to get everything ready to display, but it's time-consuming cleaning and polishing. And if I'm going to put some stock on consignment with my friend in Great Falls. . ." She shook her head and murmured, "I need a miracle."

"Will I do?" he asked gently.

She straightened, blinked, and suddenly grinned. "Miracles come in all shapes and sizes." She handed him a pot of cleaning compound and a soft rag. "This lantern will sell well as soon as it's polished."

They polished brass and scrubbed glass. They brushed and patched. They catalogued and priced. And they talked.

"You're going to gloat when I tell you this." He worked on a brass bed lamp. "I was really hurt when Aunt Millie didn't come for me." It was the first time he'd freely admitted it.

She didn't smile. He'd give her credit for that. She didn't even look happy about it. "Ace, I am so sorry. It was so un-necessary. I mean, if they wouldn't let you live with her, they could have at least let you visit."

"Or told me what happened." He couldn't keep the bitter-ness from his voice.

"I know. All those years of thinking she didn't care." She

lifted a cut-glass vase to the light. "That looks better." She picked up its mate and began meticulously cleaning every line. "I'm so glad you found the truth." Pausing, she studied him. "It helps, doesn't it?"

"It does." But not half as much as the way Nicole and her family welcomed him into their hearts. In fact, the whole community seemed set on drawing him into its midst. At ball games people talked to him as if he'd lived there all his life. Many came up to him and offered condolences on Aunt Millie's passing. Often they shared a fond memory of his aunt, making her seem more alive than he'd thought of her since he'd been abandoned. Strange. A few weeks ago he would have considered the whole business invasive, but now he discovered it consoled like a healing balm. He thought he'd put the bitterness and anger behind him years ago, but now he realized it had gone underground like a boil below the surface. The kindness of Nicole, her family, and a community of strangers had excised the infection. And something happened deep inside his soul—he wasn't ready to call it faith or trust or acceptance of God, but it was something as real as the greetings of Aunt Millie's friends.

They worked late into the night. Nicole was determined to get ready as much as she could to take to Great Falls. They arranged to leave right after breakfast the next morning.

&

Nicole studied Ace's strong yet gentle hands on the steering wheel. He'd been a good friend these past few weeks when her insides felt shaky. Mentally she clung to his support. She knotted her fingers together to stop herself from reaching out to touch his hands, seeking comfort from a physical contact.

Ace drove with casual concentration on the narrow, quiet

road. She shifted her gaze away and looked out the window at the green grain fields and golden pastures. Rough rock-banded buttes rose from the fields. Dark-green trees lined the river in the distance and always the serene, blue mountains as a backdrop. She settled back, soothed by the calm beauty of the landscape.

Ace made his way through traffic past the statue of Charlie Russell and his horse to the brass doors of the Montana Building in the heart of historic downtown Great Falls and pulled to a stop. "I get off here. You take the truck and visit your Gallery friend. Meet me back here in two hours."

He touched her chin, dropped a quick kiss on her cheek, and hurried away, briefcase in hand.

She slid behind the wheel and headed around the block to the Western Gallery, owned by her friend Brian.

Brian agreed to take most of what she'd brought. They settled on prices and commissions. He signed the papers then shoved them across the desk to her and leaned back. "There're a lot of rumblings about a woodcarver out your way. Seems he has a real treasure trove of goodies and might be selling lock, stock, and barrel. Know anything about it?"

Nicole signed the last of the papers before she answered. "Read something about it in the arts column a few weeks ago." She wasn't about to say more.

"Have you seen any of his work?"

She couldn't lie. "I have."

"Is it as good as they say?"

She rose and looked over the half wall to the store below. "Depends on what they say."

"Maybe I should pay this place a visit. Might be worth getting the whole kit and caboodle. You know how it is—if you have sole rights to someone's work, you corner a large portion of the market."

"I know how it is." She wanted to corner that market. But time was running out, and she didn't have a quarter of the money she needed. Her whole insides ached at her quandary. She wanted to believe God would provide the funds but realized how selfish it sounded. Not that she didn't think He cared. She knew He did. But wasn't she always telling Carrie that God gave her a brain to use? And Nicole's brain told her she was avoiding the obvious answer—borrow from the bank.

But her fears were stronger than her common sense. "I appreciate your taking these things for me."

He picked up a cranberry carnival glass bowl and held it to the light. "We'll both benefit. This stuff sells like hotcakes."

She glanced at her watch. "I have to go."

On the way back, she considered her options. If someone from the city drove out and offered Arman and his wife cash on the spot, would they feel obligated to wait for Nicole? Would it make any difference if they did? She didn't have the slightest chance of raising the money in time.

Ace stepped out of the doors as she stopped at the curb. She slid over, and he got in.

"Finished your work?" he asked.

"Yes." She couldn't keep the worry from her voice.

"You don't sound very pleased. What's wrong?"

She explained it to him.

"You know what I think."

"I know. Borrow from the bank. I can't bring myself to do it."

They stopped at a red light, and he slanted her a look.

"What?" she asked at his probing stare.

"I'm just wondering what it would take for you to see it isn't a risk—"

"Borrowing money is always a risk."

"Okay. Maybe what I mean is it's an acceptable risk."

His look was rife with meaning. Her thoughts swirled. Was he talking about the shop or something more? The traffic began to move, and he turned his attention away. She looked out the window, but her thoughts took a journey of their own. No doubt he noticed how she kept him at arm's length. She told herself he had to turn to God before she would allow herself to be interested. But even after he'd confessed he was learning to trust God again, she kept him at bay. Although part of her yearned to be comforted in his arms, she held back. His job, his love of adventure, all the things he had become were foreign and frightening. She wouldn't let herself consider him as more than an old friend on a quick visit.

He stopped again at a red light, looked across at a nearby car, and stiffened. Nicole peered past him but didn't know the driver of the other vehicle.

Ace suddenly switched lanes and made the next right turn.

She laughed at his sudden burst of speed. "Where are we going?"

He shrugged. "It's a surprise." He kept glancing in the rearview mirror. She turned around to see what held his interest.

"What is it?" She saw only traffic—nothing out of the ordinary.

"I thought someone was following too close."

She looked again. Of course they were close. They were in downtown Great Falls.

He turned again, heading back the way they'd come. "Did you forget something?"

He shook his head. "Changed my mind about where we're going. On second thought, where would you like to go? What would you like to do?"

She wanted to go home and get more pieces ready to display, but she owed Ace a few minutes of free time. Suddenly the idea of some quiet appealed. "I'd love to go to Gibson Park and wander around. It always refreshes me."

He made his way to the park and stopped, glanced over his shoulder as he pushed open his door, then took a long look to his right and left. "Ace, who are you looking for?"

"Nobody."

They wandered past the stained-glass display depicting the park, meandered through the brightly colored, scented flower display. She led him toward the duck pond, sat down, closed her eyes, and let the splash of the fountains and the noisy gabble of the geese and gulls ease away the tension that had become her constant companion.

Ace took her hand. She let herself relax against him, her head on his shoulder. He pressed his chin to the top of her head. "This is nice."

"Umm." She didn't know if he meant the pond or sitting so close, quiet and content. For now she didn't care. She let peace fill her.

Suddenly Ace leapt to his feet, grabbed her hand, and strode away so fast she had to trot to keep up. "Ace, what on earth?"

"Come on." He didn't slow down until they were back at the parking lot. He gave a long look over his shoulder then practically ran toward the car.

She jerked her hand from his and stopped. "What is this all about?"

He looked past her and relaxed. "Sorry." He laughed. "I thought I saw someone I didn't want to talk to. He's gone now."

"So much for a peaceful interlude," she murmured.

"Sorry." He reached for her hand. "Do you want to go home?"

Oddly she no longer did, but she nodded and followed him to the vehicle.

nine

Weary to the marrow of her bones, Nicole locked up the store. It had been a good day. Two busloads of tourists practically cleaned off the shelves. She barely got them restocked before a carload of seniors came. They weren't interested in antiques but bought one of her more pricey paintings.

It had been a productive day. And a profitable one. She'd done a quick tally before she left the store. But she knew without totaling that by the time she paid her bills and Rachel's salary and gave Ace what she owed him from the sale of Aunt Millie's stuff, she'd barely made a dent in what she needed.

When was she going to get her miracle?

She plodded home, too tired to care that it was a beautiful evening. She crossed the street, took the walkway around the side of the house, and paused when she saw Ace playing catch with Carrie.

"You're a great ballplayer." Ace tossed the ball to her.

Nicole groaned. She'd missed Carrie's game tonight.

"Put your body into it more," Ace said. "Follow through." Carrie tossed the ball. Ace caught it. "Good job."

"I've had enough." Carrie ran toward the deck, plopped down next to Gram's old chair where Gram sat with a book open on her lap, watching the other two. Nicole had noticed before that more and more of Gram's books remained on her lap; she felt a stab of guilt. She needed money for Gram's surgery. She needed money for Arman's carvings. In theory, buying the latter would bring the former within easier reach. In reality, neither seemed accessible anymore.

Ace dropped the ball and glove into the storage chest on the patio and sat beside Carrie. "Your flowers are nice," he said to Gram.

"Thank you. I find them cheerful."

Nicole hung back, watching her family, feeling distant from them. She'd been putting in such long hours at the store that she'd barely had time to eat with them for days. But Ace seemed to spend every evening with them. The irony of the situation didn't escape her.

She was about to join them when Carrie turned to Gram. "Gram, did you ever wish you'd lived someplace besides here?"

Gram stroked Carrie's blond hair. "No. This is where I found love."

"You might have found love somewhere else."

Gram chuckled. "Then I would have gone there and been happy."

"But didn't you ever want to travel? Wasn't there something you wanted to see? Like Egypt or Paris or Australia?"

Gram didn't answer right away, and Nicole waited for her reply. "Child, life offers us all sorts of options and challenges. The trick is to know which ones to pursue and then be content with our choices. God promises to guide us. And no matter what we decide, His love is ever present."

Carrie sighed. "I want to see the world."

Nicole remembered she'd once dreamed of seeing Italy. Finding her father's family. Visiting the places Mom talked about, stories she'd repeated from Nicole's father. But Nicole grew up, took on helping Gram raise Carrie, and now she had so many responsibilities she no longer had room for dreams. No, she amended. She now had different dreams.

"Ace, you know what I mean, don't you?" Carrie said. "There's so much out there to see for yourself."

Ace nodded. "There's lots to see all right, but don't think it can take the place of family and home and being part of a community like you have here."

The heat of the earlier part of the day seemed to pool inside Nicole's chest where it crowded her lungs so they couldn't work. This was Ace talking, defending family and home? She wanted to grab his arm, pull him around until she could peer in his face, and demand an explanation. A trickle of caution made her take a deep breath. Just because he defended family didn't give her reason to think he planned to stay. And when he left, could they again be happy being just the three of them? Could she?

Carrie bounced to her feet. "I never thought I'd hear you talking like Gram and Nicole." She spun around. "Oh, hi, Nicole. You're just in time to join in a home-is-everything discussion. Count me out." She swung away in disgust and went indoors.

Ace got to his feet and smiled down at Nicole. "Here's the workaholic."

"Glad you're home." Gram pushed to her feet. "I think I'll go inside, too. I need to put my feet up."

Ace took Nicole's hand and led her toward Gram's chair. When she sat down, he pulled another chair close. "You look tired."

Nicole laid her head back. "I am tired. The shop was busy."

"So you're making money hand over fist?"

She didn't want to talk about work. It discouraged her. She

wanted to know his plans. She had to make sure no one in her family got hurt. "Ace, you fit into our family so well. Both Gram and Carrie enjoy your company." She sat up and fixed him with a demanding look. "But what happens when you leave? How will we pick up the pieces?"

Ace took her hands between his and studied her face before he answered. "Like Gram says, there are options."

"Like what?" She wouldn't allow herself to dream up options to her liking.

He tapped the back of her hands with his thumbs and smiled. "Remember what the preacher said a few weeks ago about running from God's love?"

She nodded, though she wasn't sure what Sunday or which sermon he referred to.

"He asked us how far could we run from love. He meant God's love, but I think it also applies to other kinds of love." His hazel eyes serious, he looked at her chin, her mouth, and then into her eyes, holding her gaze with the power of a steel shaft. "I feel God pulling me. I want what He offers. I'm tired of running. I want to be home."

Nicole couldn't think. Home? Love? God? "You're planning to stay here?"

He nodded slowly, thoughtfully. "It sounds like a good idea."

"What about your work?"

"I could travel, use this as a home base, or I could do consulting here." He held up his hand. "Actually I haven't really thought it out, but the idea has been growing slowly."

"I don't know what to say."

He tucked a strand of hair behind her ear, his touch making it even more difficult to think. "Don't you want me to stay?"

"Of course I do. It's just—well, so sudden. So unexpected." Which wasn't entirely true. She'd prayed for a miracle. That he'd—what? Let God back into his life? Stop running, as he said? Then she could—she closed her eyes. She could allow herself to love him?

But loving a man like Ace carried far too many risks to her family. He'd come and go, doing dangerous things. They'd worry. He could get hurt or worse. She wanted Andrew back. But he was no longer Andrew. He'd grown up into Ace, who lived a life that frightened her.

"Nicole, I want to be part of what you have here."

She looked hard into his gaze, his irises like shadowed forest ponds.

"Let me help you with the store. I want to invest in it."

"You already have with Aunt Millie's antiques."

"I want to lend you the money for Arman's woodcarvings."

"I can't let you."

He jerked back and frowned. "It's a sound business deal."

"Nothing is sure."

He studied her intensely, his expression hard, withdrawn, a striking contrast to the softness and gentleness of a few seconds ago. "Exactly. Nothing is for sure. Doing something is a risk. But not doing anything is also a risk."

"No, it's not."

"If you borrow the money, either from me or a bank, you risk having to pay it back even if the business fails. Which it's not going to. But"—he held up his hand to emphasize his point—"if you don't borrow the money and buy Arman's stock, you run a very real risk of someone else's buying it and cornering the market. And then you'll lose out on the money you could have made." He sat back obviously pleased with his argument. "See—risks on both sides. It's always like that. Risks if you act. Risks if you don't. Everything has risks. You just have to decide which ones are worth taking."

"I stand to lose a great deal if someone else buys his stock."

He leaned forward, cupped her face in his hands. "I was hoping I might be a risk you'd consider." He didn't wait for her to argue or reason or accept. Gently he stroked his thumbs along her jawline. "Think about it. And here's something to help you decide." He kissed her so sweetly, so gently, tears welled up at the back of her eyes.

❧

Two days later at supper, Nicole jumped up from the table for no apparent reason, stared at the counter then sat down again. Only to jump up again. Gram had to ask her twice how work had gone.

"Fine. Busy. Okay." She twisted her fork as she talked.

Ace studied the tension on Nicole's face. It was his fault. He shouldn't have said anything about his fledgling plans. Not until the details were worked out. But the idea had been growing with each meal he shared with the Thomas family, every hour he spent with Nicole, every time he stepped inside the church. He was tired of running, tired of being homeless, fed up with denying his belief in God, a belief that survived years of pretending it didn't exist.

But it didn't change who he was and the fact he had nothing to offer Nicole except his love. And she deserved so much more. He could offer her money to buy Arman's woodcarvings but not the security she longed for. Security for Nicole meant an absence of risks. He didn't think such a thing existed.

Carrie, oblivious to the edginess gripping at least two people sharing the evening meal, told a story about the twins trying to catch a butterfly.

Nicole stirred her salad then pushed her fork away and faced Gram. "I've decided to go ahead with the purchase of Arman's carvings." She sucked in a deep breath and rushed on. "It means I have to borrow some money. But I feel it's a wise investment."

Ace's hand stopped halfway to his mouth with a load of salad on his fork, and he stared at her. Had she decided to let him lend her the money? To trust him? Had she decided he was a risk worth taking?

"I talked to Marian at the bank today. She seemed enthusiastic about it." Nicole gave a tremulous smile.

Ace understood this was a giant step for her and buried his disappointment she hadn't come to him, accepted his offer, trusted him. But the very fact she'd taken a step involving the risk of action, rather than inaction, thrilled him. He could hardly wait to be alone with her and ask what she'd decided about him. He loved her; he wanted to share his life with her. He wanted to be here in Reliance, part of her family, for as long as God gave him. He just didn't know what shape the belonging would take. Or if Nicole would allow him to be part of what she had.

Nicole leaned toward Gram. "I'd like to use the store as collateral, but I wouldn't do it without your approval."

Gram patted Nicole's hand. "It's yours now. I trust you to make the right choices concerning it." She turned to Ace. "My Nicole has quite a head for business."

Nicole groaned. "Gram, it's not as if I run a multimillion-dollar business."

Her eyes, full of purpose and determination, met Ace's. He gave her a thumbs-up sign. Her answering smile sent ripples of pride and pleasure through him. He knew this represented a major step for her. It signified in a concrete way she'd confronted her fear of risks.

But did she see him as an acceptable risk?

ప

She'd done it. She'd flown into the mists, taken a risk. Nicole restrained the bubbling feeling in the pit of her stomach until she and Ace stood in Aunt Millie's house; then she spun around in a circle, laughing. "I'm excited and scared at the same time." She hugged him and chuckled at his amused expression. "I have you to thank for all this."

He quirked an eyebrow. "All this?" He indicated the boxes waiting to be hauled to the Dumpster and the latest batch of things he'd sorted out for her. "It's Aunt Millie you should be thanking, not me."

"Not this stuff, silly." Her insides hummed with the adventure of it. "I, Nicole Thomas, have done something I've always refused to do. I have actually gone to the bank and asked to borrow money." Her smile felt too wide for her face. "I feel as if I've stepped into a brave, new, scary future. And I have you to thank for pushing me out of my safe little world."

"And how did I do that?"

She looked up into the warmth of his hazel eyes. "You're teasing me. You know what you did. You made me see that everything involves a risk. You choose the ones worth taking." She held his gaze, searching for answers in both herself and him. He'd asked if she would consider taking a risk on him. She'd thought of it between business talk all day long. Was she brave enough to take this giant step—trusting her future to a man like Ace? Trouble was, she still couldn't separate Ace from Andrew in her thoughts. She knew Andrew. She'd loved

Andrew most of her life. But Ace wasn't Andrew.

"It doesn't change who I am, Nicole."

The question haunted her every thought. "Who are you, Ace?"

He strode to the window and stared out. He returned and took her by the arms, holding her close yet not touching anywhere but the warm spots on her shoulders. He looked deep into her eyes. "Nicole, I am a man who has known little about family. I'm a loner, a risk taker. I am probably the worst person in the world for you."

Their gazes caught and held in a look that went back eighteen years. They'd shared something special then. A connection, a bond surviving years of separation, growing and thriving in the past few weeks. She felt something with this man she'd never known with another human being. Connection? Yes. Belonging, too. But more. So much more. She couldn't even find the words to describe it, except it felt as if he completed her world.

Was he a risk worth taking?

She delved deep inside her heart for the answer and came up with a handful of fluttering butterflies. "I didn't ask who you were, but who you are. Who is Ace?" What did she want him to say? What would it take to convince her to allow her love expression? She waited for his answer, hoping it would erase her fears.

"I'm tired of running from God. I'm tired of pretending I don't want to love and be loved. I want to belong, but trusting this whole belonging business—family, community—I don't know. It's completely foreign to me."

"But isn't that what families are? Belonging, community, forever?"

He tipped his head back and stared away. His jaw hardened. "That's not been my experience."

Her throat hurt so she could hardly talk. She wanted him to believe in family and happily ever after. With her? Until he could really believe, she could not let go of her tightly held protectiveness of her family. With a jolt she realized she was protecting herself as well. From disappointment and hurt. It wasn't that she didn't know who Ace was; the problem was she did. A man who strode into dangerous situations, who commanded respect and probably fear in opponents, a man who would turn her world upside down.

He looked deep into her eyes. His gaze shivered with hazel depths.

Not until she'd somehow put to rest the remnants of fear refusing to leave the pit of her stomach could she know what she truly wanted.

ten

Nicole filled out papers for the bank loan, worked on marketing plans, and forecast expenses and income. Figuring it out on paper increased her sense of rightness in doing this.

She crowded in a visit from the local carpenter and had more display shelves built along one wall in anticipation of the carvings soon to arrive.

She bounced in and out of the office area, excitement giving her life fresh color.

Every evening Ace joined them for supper, adding an undercurrent of enjoyment to the meal. It seemed Gram and Carrie vied with each other to tell him about their day and get his comments. He always found something to joke about, or he pointed out the silliness of some of their conclusions. But especially he gave a sense of solidness to their gatherings.

Nicole smiled as she watched his kindness with Gram and his patient humor with Carrie even when she spilled a jug of water over his shirtfront. He simply grabbed a towel and sponged the moisture off and said, "Nothing so refreshing as a cool shower on a hot day." When Carrie looked as if she'd burst into tears, he flicked drops of water at her until she relaxed and giggled.

Nicole glanced around the kitchen—as familiar to her as her own skin—but no longer did the walls shut the world out. No more did she want to pull them around her and protect herself and Gram and Carrie. She had taken a step that moved her beyond the safe walls, to boldly embrace challenges and walk out into the world with strong motives. Every day she felt more confidence in her move.

She ran a comb through her hair and dabbed some perfume behind her ears. The sun shone through her bedroom window with exuberant brightness. The sky glistened with midsummer blue. A beautiful Sunday. And Ace would be walking to church with them again.

She didn't want to think any further ahead than that. She refused to acknowledge the thread of worry in the back of her mind. A couple of times Ace had mentioned he would soon be finished cleaning out the house and the word "work" came up. He hadn't said what he intended to do, and she hadn't asked. She wasn't ready to deal with his real life. She knew she wasn't being fair to Ace.

Lord, show me what to do. Help me deal with these fears.

It had become a daily, fervent prayer.

Ace accompanied them to church and gave the sermon his undivided attention.

Nicole wished she could do the same, but her thoughts kept hopping from one thing to another. Ace's growing faith. Her insurmountable caution. His work and lifestyle. Her determination to protect her family from being hurt.

She caught enough of the sermon to know it had been about God's unfailing love and care. The pastor closed his talk by asking them all to stand and read together Psalm 23. Knowing the words, she didn't need to read from the overhead. Ace's deep voice joined her, saying the words with bold confidence. She caught his gaze as they said the psalm together.

" 'The Lord is my shepherd; I shall not want. He maketh

me to lie down in green pastures: he leadeth me beside the still waters. He restoreth my soul: he leadeth me in the paths of righteousness for his name's sake. Yea, though I walk through the valley of the shadow of death, I will fear no evil: for thou art with me; thy rod and thy staff they comfort me. Thou preparest a table before me in the presence of mine enemies: thou anointest my head with oil; my cup runneth over. Surely goodness and mercy shall follow me all the days of my life: and I will dwell in the house of the Lord forever.'"

The words sank deep into her soul, erasing her fears, giving her a holy assurance. God was in control of her past, her present, and her future. She could rest in His blessed unfailing love and care.

She smiled at Ace after the words died away, let herself love him wholly.

Church over and their neighbors greeted and visited with, Nicole, Ace, Gram, and Carrie headed home, laughing and talking. She could hardly wait to be alone with Ace and tell him her decision. She loved him. He was a risk well worth taking.

As they rounded the last corner, a man blocked their path. A man with a wicked-looking knife in his hand.

"Conners," he growled. "I've been waiting for you."

Nicole felt a shock race down Ace's arm. He took her hand from where it rested in the crook of his elbow and gently pushed her behind him.

"Hello, LaRue. How are you?"

There was no mistaking the cautious, almost weary note in Ace's voice. The name LaRue sounded familiar, but Nicole couldn't remember where she'd heard it.

LaRue spat on the ground beside him. "How do you think

I am? You and your friends keep messing around with me, thinking I can't do anything about it. Well, you've got yourself another think coming."

Hearing the anger in his voice, Nicole peeked around Ace to have a look at this man.

His dark blond hair hung past his ears and pushed out at wild angles from the ring of his ball cap. He looked as if he hadn't shaved in days. But it was his eyes that frightened Nicole. Wide. Wild. Darting from Ace to the women standing behind him.

"There's more than one way to deal with oil men." LaRue's gaze met Nicole's. Something evil flickered through his eyes. She caught her breath between her gritted teeth and ducked back behind Ace. LaRue! The man the telephone call had warned Ace about. An ecoterrorist, Ace had said.

Ace crossed his arms over his chest.

"LaRue, why haven't you contacted my office? We've agreed to do the tests you wanted and pay for any damages you feel you've incurred."

The man grunted. "You think you can put me off, but it didn't take me long to track you down. I saw you in Great Falls with your pretty lady."

Nicole's eyes widened. That's what had made Ace so nervous, always checking over his shoulder, rushing her out of the park.

LaRue gave a bitter laugh. "Nice bunch of women you got there. I wonder what you'd do if old LaRue happened to run into one of them some night and sort of took a little drive with them." He chortled mirthlessly. "Maybe I'd arrange to have a little knife in my pocket. Just think what I could do to that old lady."

Nicole didn't have to look at Gram or Carrie to feel their shock. Her blood pooled in the soles of her feet as cold sweaty anger flooded through her veins. She squeezed her hands into hard fists. How dare that despicable man threaten Gram?

"I'll bet ya that pretty young one would squeal like a stuck pig if old LaRue so much as threatened to have a little fun with his knife. Sort of payback time, if you know what I mean. For all the hassles you guys put me through." The man gave a wicked snort of laughter. "And what about that dark-headed beauty hiding behind yer back? Bet you'd do anything to protect her. Hey? What about it, Conners?"

Nicole felt, as much as heard, Ace's angry grunt. Without moving he said, "Nicole, take your grandmother and sister home. Go through the yard behind me."

Nicole hesitated. Did she dare leave him to face this man alone?

"Do it now," Ace ordered.

She spun around and grabbed Gram with one hand, Carrie with the other. "Come on—let's get out of here."

Carrie hung back. "What about Ace?"

"I can look after myself," Ace said.

Nicole rushed them through the nearest yard and around the house, not caring if anyone saw them and wondered what they were doing. She raced out the gate and down the alley toward home. By the time she pushed the back door open, Gram struggled for breath. Nicole helped her to a chair.

"Carrie, call the police then make Gram some tea."

Nicole headed for the door.

"Where are you going?" Carrie asked.

"To see if Ace is okay. You look after Gram." She retraced

her steps, halting behind the hedge, hoping LaRue hadn't noticed her return.

Through the twisted branches she could see Ace standing with legs slightly spread, his arms still crossed and a look of indifference on his face. Nicole was certain it was only a pose. She couldn't imagine he felt as cool and detached as he looked.

Careful not to make any noise, she watched and listened.

"LaRue, I wish you'd called the office as we agreed. I'm sure you'd be pleased with the concessions we've offered."

LaRue grunted. "You'd like to think so, I'm sure, but the only thing that would make me happy is for you people to get off my land. And be forced to stop all the underhanded things you do."

"We've done everything we could to ensure no harm has occurred to you or your property."

LaRue spat again. "Talk is cheap. But I know about all sorts of things no one reports. No one accepts responsibilities for. This stuff has to stop. One of these days you guys will push me too much and then—" He flicked his knife in the air and made an explosive sound.

The sound reverberated up Nicole's spine. She dropped back on her heels, her limbs quivering. How long did it take for the police to answer an emergency call? Ace could be dead before they got there.

Ace's voice, calm and detached, reached her. "I don't think you want this to go any further. Why don't you meet me in Great Falls tomorrow afternoon, and we'll work out something?"

Nicole's breath shuddered over her tense nerves. She jerked her head up at the sound of sirens and leaned forward to peer again through the leaves as a cruiser skidded to a halt and a young police officer threw the door open and stood behind it, his gun leveled at LaRue. "Drop it."

LaRue dropped the knife and shot his arms over his head. The policeman edged forward, kicked the knife out of the way, slapped on handcuffs, and then ran his hands up and down LaRue's body searching for hidden weapons before escorting the man to the back of the car.

"I'll be back!" LaRue hollered. "Perhaps I'll pay a visit to those sweet little gals you've been hanging around with."

Ace strode after him and leaned over to growl through the window. "You leave them out of this. Or you'll regret the day you were born."

LaRue snorted. "Finally found something you care about, eh, Conners? Maybe now you'll understand how I feel when I see my animals dying. My babies getting sick."

"Leave them alone," Ace warned him again.

LaRue stared at Ace another moment then turned away.

Weakness shivered up Nicole's limbs, and she sank to the ground.

LaRue had threatened Gram and Carrie because of her involvement with Ace.

She loved Ace.

But her love for him had brought danger to her family. She couldn't be responsible for putting them at risk.

&

Ace opened the door and looked around the kitchen.

Gram gave a shaky smile. "Glad to see you're still in one piece," she said. "I hope you sent that man packing."

"The police have taken him away."

Carrie sprang to her feet. "What a horrid person." She

shuddered. "What did he want anyway?" She looked past him. "Where's Nicole?"

"Isn't she here?" The hair on the back of his neck tingled when Carrie shook her head.

"She went to see if you were okay."

Carefully masking his expression, he said, "I'll go get her." He waited until the door shut him from their view before he broke into a run, sweat beading his brow. Had LaRue escaped and found her?

He skidded to a stop on the sidewalk and looked around. Nothing. No vehicle, save those normally parked along the street. Not a sound that didn't belong.

He took a slow deep breath. *Think, man. Where is she? Don't let LaRue's threats get to you. He's in jail right now. He can't do anything. Besides, he just wants a few thousand bucks to add to his bank account. He'd never harm anyone. He doesn't have the guts to face the consequences.*

He continued silently trying to convince himself as he strode down the sidewalk. But his mind conjured up images of LaRue's knife with a drop of blood on the tip. Nicole's blood.

"Nicole," he called. Nothing he'd faced to this moment prepared him for the panic shafting through his heart. If she had been hurt—

A soft moan to his left. He spun toward the sound.

"Where are you?" He crashed into the yard, saw her, and raced to her side.

Tears streaked her face. Her eyes had a tortured look.

"Are you okay? What's the matter?" He knelt at her side and reached for her, but she pushed his arms away.

"That man threatened my family."

"I know. He's in custody right now. He'll never hurt you."

He sat back on his heels waiting for her to calm.

Her expression grew fierce. "Can you guarantee that?"

"Of course I can't guarantee it."

"Exactly." She pushed to her feet, shoving aside the hand he extended to help her.

His insides felt like cold glass as their eyes met and he felt her shattering anger.

"I'm not willing to gamble my family against a crazy man."

He held his ground in front of her. "What are you saying?"

A shudder raced across her shoulders. "I will not put Gram and Carrie at risk. For anything."

He crossed his arms over his chest as he continued to block her escape. She'd been understandably frightened by the encounter with LaRue, but there'd never been any real danger. He had to convince her of it. "I'll talk to LaRue. I'm certain he'll be adequately mollified by the concessions we're prepared to offer him."

She lifted her chin and met his look squarely. "How nice for him."

Her response confused him. What did she want? "I don't believe he ever constituted a risk to any of us." Then why was he so afraid when he didn't know where Nicole was?

"As you yourself said, you can't guarantee it."

Anger and frustration drowned out caution and calm. "Life doesn't come with a fail-proof guarantee. Bad things happen all the time. A tree could fall on you. A fire burn down your house." At her look of fear he wished he had found another example. "But it's not likely. You can't walk around trying to anticipate and avoid any eventuality."

Her eyes blazing, she tilted her chin higher. "I know I can't predict the future. I know I'll have to deal with difficult situations. I've done so in the past. But"—she blinked hard—"I will not knowingly take risks that threaten my family's security."

He should have seen it coming. He should have known better than to open up his heart. Fool that he was. Fool.

"And I'm too great a risk? Is that what you mean?"

For a moment she hesitated then nodded. "You have enemies. You do dangerous work. It's too great a gamble."

"*I'm* too great a gamble, you mean." He'd known it all his life, so why did it sting like acid? He silenced the crying of his heart and bolted back the feelings he'd allowed to surface after a lifetime of holding them at bay.

She faced him squarely, uncertainty flickering across her face. He hesitated, willing her to change her mind. Then her expression hardened, and he knew her decision before she uttered the words that stopped the blood flowing to his heart.

"I'm sorry. I can't make any other choice."

He lifted his hand, wanting to touch her one more time; but she drew back, and he dropped his arm to his side. It was over. Big surprise. He allowed himself one more lingering look at her sad face and dark eyes then quelled any regrets.

"Good-bye then. Nice knowing you and all that stuff." He had his job. He'd keep busy. Life would go on. He spun on his heels and marched away, rigid self-control stiffening his spine.

He slammed into the house and poured himself a cup of cold coffee.

⁂

Nicole couldn't remember returning home. Her world had turned black and empty.

"Where's Ace?" Carrie demanded, as Nicole closed the door behind her.

"Where have you been?" Gram asked then, after a look at Nicole's face, added, "What's happened? You look terrible."

"Where's Ace?" Carrie asked again. "I'm starving."

"We'll go ahead without him," Nicole said, her voice quivering noticeably.

"I can wait. I'm not that hungry," Carrie said.

Nicole dropped to a chair. "He's not coming."

"Not coming?" Carrie looked as if Nicole had said the sun wouldn't rise tomorrow. "Why not?" She gasped. "Oh, no. He's been hurt, hasn't he? Where is he?" She had her hand on the doorknob before Nicole's words stopped her.

"He's not hurt. He's fine. Probably having lunch right now over at Aunt Millie's house."

Gram leaned forward. "Child, what's happened?"

The kindness of Gram's voice almost undid Nicole's rigid control of her emotions. She took a shuddering breath before she could speak. "Ace won't be coming over anymore."

Carrie bristled. "Why not?"

"I don't want to see him anymore." *Please, please don't make me say more. My insides are bleeding out through my pores. I don't know if I can remain sane long enough to deal with this.*

Give it up, Nicole, she scolded herself. *You've made the right choice. Family first. These are the two most important people in the world. This is what matters.*

"Are you crazy?" Carrie demanded. "After he saves us from that man. After all he's done, you don't want to see him?" She glared at Nicole. "You are crazy."

Nicole couldn't look at her sister. She couldn't answer her accusations.

"Well, I don't care. I want to see him again, and I will." She flounced from the room.

Nicole continued to stare at the tabletop, aware of a waiting silence. Finally she faced Gram.

"What really happened?" Gram asked.

"Things would never work out for us."

"You aren't overreacting to that little scene out there, are you? I think Ace handled himself and that man very well."

Nicole hid the guilt she felt as she shook her head. "I'm just facing reality."

"As long as you're being fair to Ace." Gram studied her carefully. "And yourself."

"I'm doing what I know is right." Her own aching desires didn't count when she knew they put Gram and Carrie in danger.

Carrie refused to join them for dinner. Nicole had little appetite and mostly rearranged her food on the plate.

She was thankful Gram ate a little and refrained from saying more about the situation.

❧

Sweat soaked Ace's shirt. He yanked it over his head and snatched a clean one off the bed.

Racing up and down two flights of stairs and out to the Dumpster all day left him tired. Dust settled on his skin. Cobwebs tangled in his hair. Amazing how much stuff Aunt Millie had packed under the eaves. But he'd managed to clean it out.

He wiped at his face and arms with his drenched shirt. Too bad his frantic efforts hadn't succeeded in keeping his thoughts at bay.

Three days since Nicole had informed him he didn't fit into her tidy little life. Three torturous days of trying to convince himself it was over and he didn't care.

He slipped his hand under his shirt and rubbed the scar on his right side. A souvenir of the one time he hadn't talked his way out of a confrontation without incurring a little damage. He pressed his fingers into the soft flesh and wondered what Nicole would think if she saw the spider-shaped scar.

He knew her reaction.

Too risky. Too risky.

The words chanted through his brain with the sound of a hundred schoolboys taunting him. All his own voice.

He curled his hand into a fist and ground it into his side.

Seems all his life he had ached for love and belonging. A family like the one Nicole cherished.

But who could blame her for not wanting a man like him?

The house was stifling. He spun on his heels and hurried outside.

The evening air was blessedly cool and fragrant from Gram's flowers next door. He settled on the wooden steps, leaning his elbows on his knees. Quiet fell around him.

He jerked his head up. "Nicole?" He couldn't see her. Or hear her. But he sensed her presence.

Only the fluttering of a bird in the branches answered his call, but he knew she was close by.

"Can we talk?" he asked softly.

For a moment he thought she would refuse; then he heard the soft padding of her footsteps coming in the back gate. He rose slowly. She stopped a few feet from him. It was too dark for him to read her expression, so he led her inside.

At the sight of her beautiful eyes he forgot he'd decided he didn't care. With aching arms he reached for her.

She shook her head and moved away.

He dropped his hands to his side. His words slow, he said,

"You're the one who made me believe I could be loved. Until you did, I was happy enough making my way through life without love."

Seeing the flicker of regret in her eyes, he allowed himself to think she could change her mind.

"I love you, Ace. But—"

He didn't let her finish. Steely fingers dug at his heart, snatching away hope. "But? I've heard it all my life. We love you, but. You're too old. You're too difficult. You're too big." As if he could help that he'd grown early but awkwardly. All hands and feet that tangled themselves together making him clumsy. "I thought you were different. I thought you'd be the sort of person who could love regardless. Regardless of flaws and imperfections." He clamped his teeth together. He would not say more. He would not turn this into a pity party.

"Ace, I do love you." Her eyes were wide and dark, begging for him to understand.

All his life he'd ached to hear those words. But especially these last few weeks. And even more so since he'd opened up his heart to loving her.

He didn't understand her resistance, and he would not let her off so easily. "Yeah, right. If there's one thing I've learned, it's that words are easy." If she wanted absolution she'd have to find it at church.

"I can't think only of myself," she insisted. "I have to consider what's best for my family."

"You're not thinking about what's best for anyone. Not Gram, not Carrie, and especially not yourself. Your father acted foolishly when you were a child, and you've never gotten over it. You think you can insulate yourself from anything that threatens the narrow little walls you've built around yourself."

He saw the shock in her face, but he couldn't stop. It poured out as if the words had a life of their own. "Sooner or later your walls will come tumbling down."

Her hand pressed to her mouth, she turned to the door.

"And I'm not your father. I would never carelessly do something to hurt you. Or your family."

The door shut behind her.

"I am not your father," he muttered then whispered softly, "I love you." But in the silence, something inside him died.

He poured a cup of coffee, not even flinching when the hot liquid overflowed on his thumb.

He would not allow regrets. He would not waste time wishing for what might have been.

Nicole was right. Family should count above everything else. For one brief, delicious, stupid moment he'd allowed himself to think he could belong to that elusive, elite group—those people who joined arms in unity. Family. Love. Belonging.

He slammed his cup down.

It was time to get on with his life.

He reached for the phone and made several calls.

eleven

"Gal, you've been sitting there doodling for an hour." Rachel's voice startled Nicole from her thoughts. "Why don't you just go find that man and say you're sorry?"

"I was thinking about the store," Nicole said. She wasn't thinking about Ace. She'd put him out of her mind.

"Yeah." Rachel snorted. "And I'm the cat's whiskers." She tapped her fingertip on the paper before Nicole. The word "Ace" had mysteriously been scribbled all over it. Nicole snatched the paper away and crumpled it into the garbage.

"It's not what you think."

Rachel perched on the corner of the desk. "And what do I think?"

Nicole shot her friend a look dripping with disdain. "I know you. You think a person should plunge into life without thinking about the consequences."

"Nope. Wrong. But I do think a person can be just a wee bit too concerned with 'what if.' "

Nicole rose to her feet. "What if I tell you to butt out?"

Rachel shrugged and followed Nicole up the stairs to stand in front of a display. "Oh, I'd listen real good. Like I always do."

Nicole grunted. Rachel had never in her whole life listened to a thing Nicole said if it disagreed with her own direction of thinking. "Guess I'd be expecting a bit much, wouldn't I?"

The day finally ended, and Nicole plodded home determinedly keeping her gaze on the cement cracks in the sidewalk as she passed Aunt Millie's house. It should be getting easier to slip by without listening for sounds of Ace inside. Without holding her breath so she wouldn't catch the scent of his maleness. Pretending she didn't strain to hear if he sang his favorite Elvis songs or played the radio. Telling herself repeatedly she would get over him.

Out of the corner of her eye a fresh post caught her attention, and she gaped at a FOR SALE sign. She stared at the words as if hoping they'd disappear. Then she spun about and looked at the blank windows. The house stood forlorn and empty. She knew he was gone.

She gasped for breath, wrapped her arms across her chest, and moaned. It was over. She sucked in trembling breaths and waited for the sickness in her stomach to end. Her knees wobbly as cooked spaghetti, she shivered toward home.

It was over. Really over. Time to get on with her life. Now she could settle back to normal without the constant temptation of knowing he was close.

"He's gone." Carrie didn't wait for Nicole to close the door before facing her with accusations. "It's all your fault. You chased him away." She turned her back but not before Nicole caught the glint of tears in her eyes.

"I'm sorry, Carrie, but I can hardly go out with a guy just because you like him, now can I?" She squeezed the younger girl's shoulders hoping to make her laugh, but Carrie shrugged away.

"Don't pretend you didn't like him, too." She glared at her sister. "You're just scared."

Nicole laughed. "Scared? Of what?"

Carrie's eyes narrowed. "You don't want to grow up. In fact, sometimes I think I'm more grown up than you are. I'm ready to accept change, but you want to keep everything nice and safe and predictable."

Nicole stared at her, startled Carrie could so easily misinterpret Nicole's motives.

"That's why you dumped Ace." Carrie nodded. "He wouldn't be part of your nice little world." She looked satisfied with her assessment. "Maybe you should grow up."

The phone rang. Carrie glared at Nicole a second longer then hurried to pick it up.

Nicole took a deep, settling breath before she faced Gram who'd silently watched the whole scene.

Nicole laughed gently. "She'll discover far too soon that life isn't as simple as she'd like it to be."

Gram's expression didn't change. "I expect she's already discovered that. Life hasn't been easy for her either."

Nicole turned away, feeling she'd been attacked by both Gram and Carrie when she'd expected support and approval.

But what did it matter as long as she did what was best for them all?

❧

Several days later Marian called from the bank to let Nicole know the papers were ready to sign for her loan.

After she hung up the phone, Nicole sat staring at the top of her desk.

Rachel hurried past to collect some brochures to hand out to the departing busload of seniors. She paused. "Bad news?"

Nicole sighed. "No. The loan papers are ready."

"Well, then, I guess it's good news. You can get those lovely carvings in before the tourist season peters out."

"I can hardly wait."

She knew from the puzzled look Rachel gave her as she

hastened back to the counter that her voice lacked enthusiasm. Enthusiasm seemed a thing of the past.

Truth was, Ace had persuaded her to seek a bank loan for the merchandise. Something she'd vowed she'd never do. Now that the loan had been approved, did she want to go ahead with borrowing the money?

Nicole rested her forehead in her palms. She'd told herself over and over she'd get used to the emptiness Ace's departure left. Again and again she recited it was for the best.

But life had lost its flavor, and she didn't know how to get it back.

Reaching into her pocket, she fingered the key Gram had given to her with instructions from Ace to clean out the antiques he'd left. She hadn't done it yet. Suddenly she made up her mind.

"Rach," she called as she hurried out, "I'll be back later."

At Aunt Millie's house she was almost overwhelmed with the smell of stale coffee and dust. And although she tried to pretend it wasn't so, the scent of Ace's aftershave lingered in every corner, triggering memories she wanted forgotten. . . had to forget if she was to get on with her life.

She hurried to the dining room to attend to business. But as she examined the antiques, memories flooded her mind. Ace leaning against the doorway watching her. The expression on his face when he found the little ceramic dog. The dawning of hope when they discovered the letters and cards from Aunt Millie. The night they'd kissed for the first time.

Tears stinging her eyes, she gathered up an armload of stuff and hurried out to the car to set the lovely lamps, the fine bone china teapot, and the pair of figurine bookends on the backseat of the car.

She leaned her head against the top of the car and forced back the pain shafting through her limbs.

She missed Ace.

She'd been missing him all her life.

Straightening, she forced a deep breath into her aching lungs.

Somehow she'd managed to survive quite comfortably all these years. She just had to focus on the right things. Like taking care of Gram and Carrie. Running her store efficiently. Finding the right things to stock her shelves with.

Right now she had these beautiful antiques of Aunt Millie's to clean and display. Life would go on. In a few days she could have Arman's woodcarvings if she went ahead with the loan.

She would learn to put these few weeks with Ace in proper perspective. A childhood dream with no place in her adult reality.

Gathering calmness about her like a cloak, she marched back to the house to collect more things. But the memories of Ace were too overpowering. She clutched a cubical paperweight in one hand and a brass candelabra in the other and hurried out, locking the door behind her.

At the store she carried the items into the back room and set them on her worktable then stepped away to admire them. She pulled a wide ledger toward her and began to catalogue each item, noting what she considered a fair purchasing price then what she hoped to be the selling price.

That done, she got cloths and polish from a shelf and set to work cleaning the brass.

Rachel entered the room. She picked up each item and exclaimed over it then sat on a stool and watched Nicole work.

Nicole concentrated on her job. She had almost forgotten the other woman's presence until Rachel said, "You can't scrub out memories, you know."

"Just bringing out the best in this lovely old brass." She held it up to the light. "It takes a lot of work to get the tarnish from around these little grape leaves." She found a toothbrush and bent over to work on the design.

"Oh, come on, Nicole. You're so focused you're driving me nuts. Talk to me, gal. What's going on?"

Nicole shot her a startled look. "I'm cleaning brass. What's the problem?"

"You might fool some of the people all of the time and all of the people some of the time, but you can't fool me. I can practically read your mind."

Knowing it was true, Nicole didn't take her eyes off the candlestick holder. If Rachel so much as glimpsed her face she'd know Nicole's thoughts had slid back to Aunt Millie's house and the man who'd resided there so recently.

"Okay. Don't look at me. It doesn't matter. So you've told this man to get out of your life. Now what are you going to do?"

"What else could I do?" She scrubbed at a corner so vigorously she sprayed cleaning compound all over the tabletop. "You know what happened. That man threatened Gram and Carrie."

"Wasn't there. Can't argue with that. But, hey. We hear about random acts of violence every day."

"Not in Reliance." She wiped the spots off the table and continued more slowly.

"Maybe not. But it seems to me you're punishing Ace for something that wasn't his fault."

"It's not that simple."

Rachel leaned her back against the shelves and planted her feet on the table.

"Huh. Life never is. It throws you curve balls all the time. But sometimes it's better to catch one of those curve balls than to keep ducking."

Nicole shuddered. "Sounds dangerous. Guess that's why I never got into playing baseball."

"It isn't just playing ball you've avoided for fear of getting hurt." Rachel dropped her feet to the floor and planted her hands on her thighs as she leaned close to Nicole. "You avoid everything that hints of risk."

Nicole kept her attention on the candelabra even though she'd practically polished it to death.

"And this is bad because?"

Rachel leaned back again. "Because, dear girl, you won't let yourself see the possibilities—the adventure. The thrill of a fuller life."

"You sound like a pop psychology major. What would you have me do? Live life in the fast lane?"

"Nothing as rash as that. But what would be wrong with grabbing and enjoying all the goodness and beauty that come your way?" She paused then added, "Even if the whole idea frightens you."

"You're saying I'm scared?" Nicole glared at Rachel.

"Aren't you?"

Her friend's soft words annoyed her even more than her insinuations. "Not at all. Besides, what's there to be scared of?"

Rachel narrowed her eyes and gave Nicole a stern look. "Maybe of trusting someone. Letting yourself care enough about them even when their choices could hurt you." She held up her hand stopping the words Nicole had been about to release. "And I'm not talking about Gram and Carrie." She paused and gave Nicole another hard look. "It's time you came to grips with your feelings about your father."

Nicole's head jerked up. "What are you talking about?" What was it with everyone thinking this had to do with her father?

"Think about it. You should be able to connect the dots."

The bell over the door sounded, signaling a customer.

Rachel headed for the door. "I'll get it." She paused. "Nicole, sometimes it seems you're so afraid of being hurt you're going to miss out on the best life has to offer. Just think about it. Okay?"

Nicole scrubbed at the brass. She didn't want to think about it. But Rachel's words upset her carefully constructed arguments. She set aside the candelabra and stared at her blackened fingers.

She always considered family when making decisions. Doing what was best for them was her first concern.

Wasn't it?

This wasn't about her father.

It was about family.

Her only concern had been to save Gram and Carrie from the disappointment and pain she'd felt when her father abandoned her to pursue other interests.

Okay, so strictly speaking, that wasn't what happened. He hadn't abandoned her. He died. Doing something he didn't have to, taking an unnecessary risk. It felt like abandonment.

And I never want to feel that way again.

Her thoughts twirled in knots. Jumping to her feet, she scrubbed her hands clean then called to Rachel, "Close up if I'm not back in time."

She drove around town growing more and more confused. Finally, in desperation, she headed home. Maybe she would find the peace she ached for in the shelter of its four walls.

Gram looked up from her TV program and checked the time on the clock over the door as Nicole entered. "You're early today."

Nicole nodded. "Can I make you some tea?"

"That would be nice."

Gram made small talk as Nicole filled the kettle and waited for it to boil.

"What really brings you home in the middle of the afternoon?" Gram asked when Nicole settled beside her with a cup of tea for each of them.

Nicole smiled. "Can't fool you, can I?"

Gram patted Nicole's hand. "Growing old has some advantages, and one of them is that I've learned to see when someone I love is troubled. It's Ace, isn't it?"

"I'm so confused."

Gram waited patiently as Nicole sorted through her thoughts, trying to verbalize her turmoil.

"Rach thinks I'm afraid to let myself love someone because I feel my father abandoned me."

Gram nodded, her expression thoughtful. "Rachel has known you a long time."

Nicole nodded. "Almost forever." But did that give her the right to evaluate Nicole's thoughts?

Gram continued. "No doubt you've shared lots of secrets."

"Like maybe she can see things about me I can't see for myself?"

"What do you think?"

Nicole shook her head. "I don't know what to think. I

vowed I would never do anything to hurt you or Carrie."

"Child, you have been such a comfort to me, but don't you realize if you throw away your own happiness on my account it would hurt me very deeply? Carrie wouldn't want it either."

"I know." Gram's words didn't ease the tension eating at Nicole's nerves.

"You know Ace isn't a risk to our happiness, don't you, child?"

She nodded even though she wasn't sure she agreed.

Gram squeezed Nicole's hand. "This isn't about us. It's about you. What do you want? What do you need? Allow yourself to be happy."

Nicole hugged Gram. "Thanks." She glanced at the clock. "You sit and watch TV while I make supper for a change."

She made everyone's favorites. Fried chicken for Carrie, mashed potatoes and gravy for Gram. And apple crisp for dessert—a favorite for all of them.

Carrie gave her a suspicious look, but she must have seen something in Nicole's expression that kept her from reiterating the words she'd spoken every meal since Ace had left. Words of accusation about driving Ace away.

Nicole barely spoke throughout the meal, trying to sort out her feelings. And later, as she lay in bed, she tried to make sense of the confusion in her heart and mind.

Did her happiness matter? Wasn't that selfish? Or was she using Gram and Carrie as protection against getting hurt?

Pain stabbed through her. A reminder of the pain she'd felt when her father died. She'd loved him so much. She used to wait at the door for his return. He'd scoop her into a bear hug then toss her in the air.

"I love you, baby," he'd say as he rumpled her hair.

She still ached for his hugs and words of love.

Why did it hurt so much more to lose him than Mom and Dad?

Because they couldn't help it. Mom and Dad had been hit by a careless driver. It wasn't their fault.

Her father had a choice. He didn't have to go skydiving.

She shook her head in the dark.

It wasn't as if he'd done it on purpose.

All sorts of people did daredevil things. He'd done it lots of times.

In fact—she sat bolt upright in bed, remembering something she'd blocked from her mind for years. He was an instructor at the skydiving school. Her mother had told her he'd died trying to save a student who panicked.

She fell back against the pillows.

How had she forgotten that?

Turning her face into the pillow, she muffled her groan. She'd blocked it from her mind because it was easier to blame him than to accept the finality of her loss.

For the first time ever, without anger or resentment, she allowed herself to weep for the loss of her beloved parent, the one she looked like, the one she'd been named for, the one she missed with an ache that would never leave.

Her pillow was soaked with healing tears when she made up her mind what she had to do. Spent from her emotional cleansing, she fell asleep.

❧

Ace stared at the flickering screen of his laptop perched on the top of the wide mahogany desk in the spacious office.

Martha, who'd been buzzing in and out of his office all morning, hovered in the doorway. "Sorry to interrupt, sir, but I have Mervin calling from Kuwait. Do you want to talk to him?"

Ace shook his head. "I still haven't decided. Tell him I'll call him as soon as I know." Kuwait. The Yukon. Offshore. Everyone seemed to want him at once.

He sank back into the leather chair. It was good to be back to work. It was where he belonged. Where he fit. That little interlude at Reliance served one worthwhile purpose—to reinforce the fact he would never love or be loved.

Through his mind flashed the memory of a shoebox with his name on it, filled with cards and letters from Aunt Millie.

It hurt to know she'd wanted him but had been denied access.

He couldn't think of Aunt Millie without picturing a dark-haired, sweet-faced little elf. But for all her talk, Nicole's belief in love and family did not extend to anyone but Carrie and Gram.

She didn't even have Aunt Millie's excuse. No one had denied her the freedom to love Ace.

He sighed. This was for the best. For his own good. Some things were just not meant to be. Not for him. Love and family were not in the works for Ace Conners.

He opened the top drawer of his desk where he'd stashed that stupid little dog he'd given Aunt Millie one dream-filled Christmas when he'd still believed love and family were possible for him.

Why had he brought it with him?

Because he couldn't bear to throw it out. He planned to pack it in his luggage to accompany him on his travels. He'd never packed one ounce more than necessary in all his years of moving and traveling, so why this pathetic ornament?

He fingered the chipped ears of the misshapen dog.

Most of his life he'd carried around the conviction no one cared. He'd blamed Aunt Millie for deserting him. A convenient excuse for the hardening of his heart.

He'd shut out God, blaming Him for not answering his prayers.

A startling, unforgiving truth faced him.

He could no longer blame someone else for the way his life had turned out.

He could no longer pretend he didn't bear some responsibility. Why hadn't he bothered to look up Aunt Millie? He could have returned to Reliance anytime in the years since he reached adulthood. He could have gone to see her.

But he hadn't.

Because, he admitted, he preferred to run away. Blaming others for what he lacked in his life had become a convenient habit.

Pushing the laptop away, he set the little dog in front of him and stared at it.

So now it came down to another choice, similar in so many ways.

He could either continue to run, or he could commit himself to the cause of finding love. Finding out if it was real and enduring. Running seemed the safest thing to do. The most familiar. Change was difficult and scary.

He stared at the dog for a long time, slowly accepting things he knew to be true.

God's love was real. He could run from it, but he couldn't deny it.

His love for Nicole was real. He could ignore that, too. Or he could be there for her, stand by until she was ready to trust his love.

He reached for the intercom. "Martha, call Mervin. I've made up my mind."

❧

Nicole hurried from the bank. She paused outside her shop and looked up at the sign.

"Grandpa's Attic has taken a big step," she whispered.

Inside, she waved the papers at Rachel. "I did it. I signed the papers for the loan."

Rachel gave her a puzzled look. "I thought it was a done deal."

"I could have changed my mind right up until this morning when I signed the papers."

Rachel shook her head. "Why would you change your mind?"

"Because it's a risk. What if I can't pay it back? What if they foreclose on the store or something?" She laughed. "Forget it." It no longer mattered. She was finished with living in a cocoon of safety. "By the way, can you look after the store by yourself a couple of days?"

Rachel's expression grew more puzzled. "I can call in one of the high school girls if I need help. Why? What are you up to?"

"I'm off to Great Falls."

"Why?"

"To find Ace."

"Why?"

"To tell him I love him. Beg him to believe me and give me another chance."

Rachel hugged her, and they laughed together.

"Good for you," Rachel said.

Nicole got to the city midafternoon. "Please still be here," she whispered. It took her several minutes to locate a parking spot. Her insides quivered with anticipation. And dread. What if he'd packed up the temporary office and moved elsewhere? What if he wouldn't talk to her? After all the disappointments and failures of love in his life she could hardly blame him if he didn't trust her now. *Lord, please let him hear me out. Forgive me for not trusting You sooner. Because You are the one who holds the future.*

Her footsteps quickened as she entered the building and headed for the stairs. She panted by the time she reached the second floor. The butterflies below her heart multiplied and fluttered rapidly. She forced herself to take slow, deep breaths.

A woman with dark-rimmed glasses, in the process of pulling a door closed behind her, glanced at Nicole. "May I help you?"

"May I speak to Ace Conners, please?"

"I'm sorry—he's not here."

Her insides froze. The butterflies died. "Can I make an appointment to see him in the morning?"

"He's closed this office. He won't be returning."

Nicole hoped her legs wouldn't let her down. "Where has he gone?"

"I'm sorry. I'm not at liberty to say."

Nicole didn't know how she managed to stumble away without collapsing. Down on the street she leaned against the wall, moaning, her shock too deep for words or tears.

It was too late. Her foolish fears had cost her the one thing she'd wanted all her life. Love. Overwhelming love.

Somehow she made her way back to her car and sat for a long while without turning the key.

It was dark by the time she pulled herself together enough to make her way out of the city.

She was thankful Gram and Carrie were in bed when she dragged herself into the house, too weary to think. Her mind numb, she fell onto her bed without removing her clothes.

She woke late the next morning with a raging headache and covered her head with the pillow.

Then it hit her. She had one more chance. The house. He must have left instructions for the real estate agent to contact him.

She jumped from bed, caught a glimpse of herself in the mirror, and shuddered. Yuk! It was enough to make her sick. She stripped off her wrinkled clothes and showered until her skin tingled. Hurrying now, anxious to get on with locating Ace, she pulled on a pair of faded jeans and a bright yellow T-shirt, pausing only long enough to smooth her hair with a brush before she raced outside and around the house to the front. She'd been afraid Gram would demand to know what she was up to, but she saw no sign of her; then Nicole remembered it was Gram's day to have tea with a bunch of her cronies.

She skidded to a halt in front of Aunt Millie's house and stared.

The FOR SALE sign was gone.

She stared at the empty spot. It must have fallen. She searched under the trees and through the tall grass. Nothing. No missing sign.

She made her way to the backyard before she collapsed in a sobbing heap on Gram's rocking chair. Why, oh, why had she been so slow to recognize what mattered in her life? Holding on to her tight-fisted security seemed vastly shortsighted now. And so empty without the one thing that mattered. Ace. She groaned his name and wrapped her arms across her stomach as if she could somehow stop the pain. But the pain ate at her until it consumed her. How would she ever survive? *Ace. Oh, Ace. How could I be so blind? I'd give anything to have another chance.*

"Nicole?"

His voice came from her agonized longings. She closed her eyes and rolled forward over her stomach to block the sound.

"Nicole, look at me."

She felt a touch. Oh, that it were real and not her tortured wishes. Pressure on her shoulder turned her. A finger tipped up her chin.

"Look at me."

She opened her eyes, squinting against the brightness of the azure blue sky.

"Ace?" She bounded from the chair, practically knocking him off his feet.

He staggered back, grinning. "Hi."

"Hi." She leaned forward trying to bring him into focus. He seemed real enough. She sniffed. It was the same trademark mixture of scents. "Where did you come from?"

He laughed. "I decided to come back."

"The FOR SALE sign?"

"I took it down. Thought I'd fix up the old house." He sobered. "Nicole, I've spent a lifetime throwing love away when all the time it was the cry of my heart. Suddenly I saw I had to grab it if I was ever to have it. I've decided to stop running. And I'm hoping I can persuade you it's safe to love me."

"You're going to find your job pretty easy."

His eyes lit with an inner glow. "What do you mean?"

"I've done some serious thinking, too. I've been hiding. Afraid to let myself love anyone as I did my father. Afraid I might be hurt again. But no more. I wouldn't want to miss the best of life because of childish fears."

He opened his arms, and she flung herself into them. It was like coming home.

The need for words was silenced by his kiss.

He tucked her into the warmth of his shoulder and turned her toward Aunt Millie's house.

"I've been busy this morning." He lifted her chin with a firm fingertip and pointed to the roof.

There, with its red nose blinking off and on, perched the reindeer that had spent so many years in the attic.

"You've come home to stay."

"This is where I found what my heart needs. I'm going to let my associates do the fieldwork. I'll do consulting work out of the house."

epilogue

Nicole stood at the door, her snow-white dress a perfect princess line. The sun shone bright and golden. Gram's flowers bloomed with joy. And waiting for her at the end of the path stood Ace, so handsome in his black tux that for a moment her knees wobbled. Carrie made her way down the path, stood across from Ace, and turned to smile at Nicole.

Rachel followed Carrie, their yellow dresses bright as the sunshine.

Two of Ace's friends stood at his side. All of them watched the door, waiting for Nicole.

She stepped out and saw no one but Ace as she slowly closed the distance between them.

"I love you," he whispered, as she took his arm and faced the preacher.

"I love you, too," she whispered back. And then they listened as the preacher exhorted them to love and trust and be true.

They had written their own vows.

Ace turned and, his voice husky, said, "Nicole, I will love you until death. I will never let anything come between us or knowingly separate us. 'Thy people shall be my people, and thy God my God.' Nothing but death shall part you and me."

Nicole smiled through her tears. They'd kept their promises secret until this moment, and the fact he'd quoted from Ruth, the same passage she'd chosen, thrilled her. She took a deep breath and, her voice quavering, said, "Andrew, Ace, I love you with my heart and life. I will trust you throughout our lives together." Her voice grew stronger as she quoted the verse she had chosen. " 'Whither thou goest, I will go; and where thou lodgest, I will lodge.' Til death do us part."

They kissed for the first time as man and wife, and the friends and neighbors who'd gathered to share this moment cheered.

Later, much later, they slipped into Aunt Millie's house, now their home. Gram and Carrie would continue to live next door until Carrie left for university next year. Nicole would be close enough to help Gram as she grew older. Ace had already set up his consulting business. But wherever he went or whatever he did in the future Nicole would be at his side.

Ace looked down at her. "I never thought this would happen. I have really and truly come home."

"I will thank God every day for bringing you back."

"Amen."

They smiled at each other, and then he lowered his head and kissed her. They had both found what their hearts desired.

A Letter To Our Readers

Dear Reader:

In order that we might better contribute to your reading enjoyment, we would appreciate your taking a few minutes to respond to the following questions. We welcome your comments and read each form and letter we receive. When completed, please return to the following:

Fiction Editor
Heartsong Presents
PO Box 719
Uhrichsville, Ohio 44683

1. Did you enjoy reading *Cry of My Heart* by Linda Ford?
   ❑ Very much! I would like to see more books by this author!
   ❑ Moderately. I would have enjoyed it more if

   _____

   _____

   _____

2. Are you a member of **Heartsong Presents**? ❑ Yes ❑ No
   If no, where did you purchase this book? _____

   _____

3. How would you rate, on a scale from 1 (poor) to 5 (superior), the cover design? _____

4. On a scale from 1 (poor) to 10 (superior), please rate the following elements.

   _____ Heroine   _____ Plot
   _____ Hero   _____ Inspirational theme
   _____ Setting   _____ Secondary characters

5. These characters were special because? _____

_____

_____

6. How has this book inspired your life? _____

_____

_____

7. What settings would you like to see covered in future
   Heartsong Presents books? _____

_____

_____

8. What are some inspirational themes you would like to see
   treated in future books? _____

_____

_____

9. Would you be interested in reading other **Heartsong
   Presents** titles?   ❏ Yes   ❏ No

10. Please check your age range:
   ❏ Under 18   ❏ 18-24
   ❏ 25-34   ❏ 35-45
   ❏ 46-55   ❏ Over 55

Name _____

Occupation _____

Address _____

City, State, Zip_____

Heart♥ong

Any 12
**Heartsong
Presents** titles
for only
$27.00*

CONTEMPORARY ROMANCE IS CHEAPER BY THE DOZEN!
Buy any assortment of twelve *Heartsong Presents* **titles and save 25% off the already discounted price of $2.97 each!**

*plus $2.00 shipping and handling per order and sales tax where applicable.

HEARTSONG PRESENTS TITLES AVAILABLE NOW:

__HP426 *To the Extreme*, T. Davis	__HP513 *Licorice Kisses*, D. Mills
__HP429 *Love Ahoy*, C. Coble	__HP514 *Roger's Return*, M. Davis
__HP430 *Good Things Come*, J. A. Ryan	__HP517 *The Neighborly Thing to Do*,
__HP433 *A Few Flowers*, G. Sattler	W. E. Brunstetter
__HP434 *Family Circle*, J. L. Barton	__HP518 *For a Father's Love*, J. A. Grote
__HP438 *Out in the Real World*, K. Paul	__HP521 *Be My Valentine*, J. Livingston
__HP441 *Cassidy's Charm*, D. Mills	__HP522 *Angel's Roost*, J. Spaeth
__HP442 *Vision of Hope*, M. H. Flinkman	__HP525 *Game of Pretend*, J. Odell
__HP445 *McMillian's Matchmakers*, G. Sattler	__HP526 *In Search of Love*, C. Lynxwiler
__HP449 *An Ostrich a Day*, N. J. Farrier	__HP529 *Major League Dad*, K. Y'Barbo
__HP450 *Love in Pursuit*, D. Mills	__HP530 *Joe's Diner*, G. Sattler
__HP454 *Grace in Action*, K. Billerbeck	__HP533 *On a Clear Day*, Y. Lehman
__HP458 *The Candy Cane Calaboose*,	__HP534 *Term of Love*, M. Pittman Crane
J. Spaeth	__HP537 *Close Enough to Perfect*, T. Fowler
__HP461 *Pride and Pumpernickel*, A. Ford	__HP538 *A Storybook Finish*, L. Bliss
__HP462 *Secrets Within*, G. G. Martin	__HP541 *The Summer Girl*, A. Boeshaar
__HP465 *Talking for Two*, W. E. Brunstetter	__HP542 *Clowning Around*, W. E. Brunstetter
__HP466 *Risa's Rainbow*, A. Boeshaar	__HP545 *Love Is Patient*, C. M. Hake
__HP469 *Beacon of Truth*, P. Griffin	__HP546 *Love Is Kind*, J. Livingston
__HP470 *Carolina Pride*, T. Fowler	__HP549 *Patchwork and Politics*, C. Lynxwiler
__HP473 *The Wedding's On*, G. Sattler	__HP550 *Woodhaven Acres*, B. Etchison
__HP474 *You Can't Buy Love*, K. Y'Barbo	__HP553 *Bay Island*, B. Loughner
__HP477 *Extreme Grace*, T. Davis	__HP554 *A Donut a Day*, G. Sattler
__HP478 *Plain and Fancy*, W. E. Brunstetter	__HP557 *If You Please*, T. Davis
__HP481 *Unexpected Delivery*, C. M. Hake	__HP558 *A Fairy Tale Romance*,
__HP482 *Hand Quilted with Love*, J. Livingston	M. Panagiotopoulos
__HP485 *Ring of Hope*, B. L. Etchison	__HP561 *Ton's Vow*, K. Cornelius
__HP486 *The Hope Chest*, W. E. Brunstetter	__HP562 *Family Ties*, J. L. Barton
__HP489 *Over Her Head*, G. G. Martin	__HP565 *An Unbreakable Hope*, K. Billerbeck
__HP490 *A Class of Her Own*, J. Thompson	__HP566 *The Baby Quilt*, J. Livingston
__HP493 *Her Home or Her Heart*, K. Elaine	__HP569 *Ageless Love*, L. Bliss
__HP494 *Mended Wheels*, A. Bell & J. Sagal	__HP570 *Beguiling Masquerade*, C. G. Page
__HP497 *Flames of Deceit*, R. Dow &	__HP573 *In a Land Far Far Away*,
A. Snaden	M. Panagiotopoulos
__HP498 *Charade*, P. Humphrey	__HP574 *Lambert's Pride*, L. A. Coleman and
__HP501 *The Thrill of the Hunt*, T. H. Murray	R. Hauck
__HP502 *Whole in One*, A. Ford	__HP577 *Anita's Fortune*, K. Cornelius
__HP505 *Happily Ever After*,	__HP578 *The Birthday Wish*, J. Livingston
M. Panagiotopoulos	__HP581 *Love Online*, K. Billerbeck
__HP506 *Cords of Love*, L. A. Coleman	__HP582 *The Long Ride Home*, A. Boeshaar
__HP509 *His Christmas Angel*, G. Sattler	__HP585 *Compassion's Charm*, D. Mills
__HP510 *Past the Ps Please*, Y. Lehman	__HP586 *A Single Rose*, P. Griffin

(If ordering from this page, please remember to include it with the order form.)

Presents

HEARTSONG PRESENTS

If you love Christian romance…

$10.^{99}$

You'll love Heartsong Presents' inspiring and faith-filled romances by today's very best Christian authors…DiAnn Mills, Wanda E. Brunstetter, and Yvonne Lehman, to mention a few!

When you join Heartsong Presents, you'll enjoy four brand-new, mass market, 176-page books—two contemporary and two historical—that will build you up in your faith when you discover God's role in every relationship you read about!

Imagine…four new romances every four weeks—with men and women like you who long to meet the one God has chosen as the love of their lives…all for the low price of $10.99 postpaid.

To join, simply visit www.heartsong presents.com or complete the coupon below and mail it to the address provided.

Mass Market 176 Pages

YES! Sign me up for Heartsong!

NEW MEMBERSHIPS WILL BE SHIPPED IMMEDIATELY!
Send no money now. We'll bill you only $10.99 postpaid with your first shipment of four books. Or for faster action, call 1-740-922-7280.

NAME_____

ADDRESS_____

CITY_____ STATE _____ ZIP _____

MAIL TO: HEARTSONG PRESENTS, P.O. Box 721, Uhrichsville, Ohio 44683
or sign up at WWW.HEARTSONGPRESENTS.COM